GROW UP!

A Self-Help Guide for Toddlers

Also by Nick Hendrie:

Business
Be Better: Interview Tips for the Unemployed and Unemployable
(self-published, available on Amazon)

Non-fiction
A Hen(drie) Party: The Birthday Memoirs of Nick Hendrie
(memoir currently being written)

Fiction
Railcard: Off Peak
(erotic-thriller set on Northwestern railways – currently seeking a publisher. Positive discussions held with Netflix about an adaption).

GROW UP!

A Self-Help Guide for Toddlers

Nick Hendrie
With Tom Ratcliffe

Published by Vulpine Press in the United Kingdom in 2023

ISBN: 978-1-83919-551-8

www.vulpine-press.com

For Mil, who said "who the f**k wants to read that?"
and Ani, for everything else.

Contents

Introduction

Stop crying! Stop sleeping! Learn to walk! Learn to talk! Take things seriously! Grow Up!

Does this sound familiar? Are you between the ages of six months and thirty months? Are you or your parents ready to take your personal and professional growth *seriously*? Then *this* is the book for you.

Throughout this lifestyle reappraisal, you'll learn that it's never too early to turn your life around. It's a competitive world out there, and both you and your parents should already be looking at giving you a leg up.

Through good fortune and careful planning, I've not had any children of my own (that's got nothing to do with my virility either; I don't care what you read or what pub toilet door you read it on). As such, my motivation is pure and transparent – I only wish to give children all the advice I wish I'd had at their age.

It's been said that children are the future. I say children are the current and/or the present.

They are the NOW.

Jobs are getting taken by robots. Or the Chinese. Or Chinese robots. There are zero-hour contracts falsifying unemployment figures. You're planning to wait until you're eighteen to make yourself employable? GROW UP!

Outside of your professional life, your personal life also needs careful tuning. I'm sorry to say but the days when your parents would find you a suitable match from a neighbouring village in exchange for a large bag of grain or a sow are long gone. People want well-rounded, normal, collected people that they can choose over the Internet. They don't want to live with a sow (even people who free animals from labs wouldn't). Do you think they'd want you? The way you are now?

You're laughable.

This book will equip you with everything you need to become a thriving human being and *crush* the competition – whether it's on the playground or in the boardroom!

As with all worthwhile things (e.g. counting the dinosaurs from each prehistoric era featured in *Jurassic Park* only to discover that the majority are from the *Cretaceous* and not the *Jurassic* period then writing letters to Steven Spielberg and Sam Neil) this book will be difficult at first to comprehend.

If you're as small-minded as my brother-in-law, you might even say it's stupid (and if you know my brother or are a fan of idioms, you'll know he's pretty black for a kettle).

Trust me. I know what I'm doing. While researching for this I read books that *aren't* this one. *GROW UP!* was written so a toddler can pick it up or have it picked up for them, read it or have it read to them, and by the end, they (you) will know how to live their (your) life to achieve their (your) potential. It is that simple. I ask that you read the book in the order it's been written. Thanks.

I take those thanks back because you should do this anyway without being asked.

Dear parents/guardians

Firstly, a massive well done to parents and guardians who have bought this book. You've birthed children (not actually that special if you think about it; all mammals reproduce that way, yet you'd never see a marmoset showing you pictures of its kids in the staff room when you're trying to make a coffee). I hope they bring you plenty of joy on your finite time left on the planet you've helped to destroy (if mainstream media is to be believed).

This book is aimed at children. It will cover the very early stages of childhood right through to adult issues like buying your first home. If you have purchased a home, then congratulations. By *you* I do mean *you* though. I've seen people celebrating on *Facebook* that they've bought a house, then it turns out they paid about 7% of the deposit and their parents are picking up the rest. You haven't bought anything. What you've done there is you've taken out a third-party loan with an unspecified rate of interest.

If you weren't related to these people, it would be a police matter.

Incidentally, if you haven't bought a home but would like to, I suggest contacting Mark Bridgers at *Goadsby Estate Agents* in Southampton. He specialises in people he calls the 'unmortgageable' and is very good (I probably would've said all that even if he hadn't asked me to).

If this book has been bought for you or your child, I understand you might feel odd. If it's your first child, then chances are it is just from someone well-meaning. However, they may be unsure about how good a parent you'll be. If you already have children and someone has bought it for you, I'd be concerned about how they perceive you as a parent. If you are co-parenting with someone and they bought it for *you*, I would genuinely be livid. Regardless, the best way to get revenge on these naysayers is by showing you *are* fit to raise a child and by raising the best, the quietest child you can and then shoving their passive aggressiveness back down their throats. Reading this book to your child is the best way to do that.

You will, certainly, in the early stages, have to read this book aloud to your child (although I could read from the age of nine months – obviously, I don't remember it but, this is what I've been told by my mother). I would suggest maybe setting them up with a pen and a pad to make notes (if old enough).

You may also find something useful to improve your own life while reading – although if you don't, that's no one's fault, least of all mine as this book is aimed squarely (through a sniper scope) at children.

Nick Hendrie

Chapter 1
Hold Your Head Up

Let's start at the beginning. Come on now. You're between six and thirty months old. Isn't it time you held your damn head up? You know – like an adult – not a simpering idiot, greedily guzzling milk like some mad goat! Be true to yourself and look life straight in the face. Don't stare at the ground like some beta-baby, bottom-feeder benefit cheat. This is your life, and you're wasting it one second at a time. 1, 2, 3, 4, 5, 6…I could go on.

Sure, your brain hasn't fully developed yet but guess what? Time doesn't care. The 24 hours you've just wasted gurgling and napping in a puddle of your own sick is exactly as important as the twenty-four that will make up your wedding one day (if you choose to get married. A lot of people don't these days, which is their prerogative. When I was younger, I wanted to get married every few years and I succeeded for a while. These days I'm less competitive about marriage. Do it if you want; I don't care. If you are going to do it, for Christ's sake make sure it's a free bar. And make the father of the bride re-draft his speech a few times).

5

Doctors were astonished when I sat bolt upright in bed at the age of one week and started reading a book (a pop-up edition of *Atlas Shrugged* by Ayn Rand). I may not have been *able* to read per se, but I was showing willing, and it's this tenacious spirit that continues to enrich my life.

Don't you want a life like mine?

I'm on first-name terms with four people who have swimming pools, I've earned enough to pay income tax for most of my career, and just this morning I ate a chicken omelette where the eggs came from the same chicken that provided the meat. And yet look at you. Unable to even hold your head upright unaided. Embarrassing.

Step One: Focus

It's pertinent to say at this juncture that it's been so long since I found lifting my head a challenge that it's difficult to advise on how to do it. It would be better if a baby/toddler wrote this section, but if you guys were capable of that then you wouldn't need this fantastic book. Nevertheless, I will do my best to advise with an all-purpose technique.

There are, obviously, any number of head-lifting styles but for the sake of ease I've chosen the simplest (I am in the early stages of discussing potential spin-offs from this book with my publishers, one of which focuses exclusively on head-lifting techniques. Nothing is yet confirmed – they said it was 'interesting'. They remain non-committal to my revolutionary request to provide 3D diagrams in the pages of this book. Providing this in the e-book version would prove 'challenging').

So, you're staring at the floor, or maybe, suffering the indignity of having some gonk hold your neck up so you can see. What now for you? Do you want to stay like this for the rest of your life? Of course not! Then it's time to *focus*. What do you want more than anything? To hold your head up unaided. How will you do it? By *focusing*.

Step Two: Technique

Perfect technique is everything, and practice makes perfect. But if you're practising the wrong technique, it doesn't make perfect, does it? No, no, it does not.

It sounds terrifying at first, but once you break it down to the composite movements it becomes incredibly easy. It's worth mentioning that I don't know a great deal about the human body and/or how it works. I don't necessarily agree with that statement, but my publisher has asked me to include it).

Anyway, back to technique. First you must stiffen the muscles in your neck. This will turn your neck into one long, rigid pole with your head at the top. Not so scary now, right? All you have to do from here is lift that pole. That is it.

To lift the neck pole that has your head at the end, you must utilise what I believe is called the neck ball. This is a joint at the bottom of your neck, where the neck is attached to the chest. The neck rotates on this ball, and you want to push your face *away* from the floor, thus lifting your head up.

Once your eyes are level with the world (use a nearby object to ascertain this – it can be anything. A signed copy of *GROW UP!* Or a gift from an estate agent that you haven't got around

7

to taking to Sue Ryder yet) you must *stop* moving your neck and hold it where it is. This might be difficult at first, but after **Step Three** it should become easier.

And there you have it. These are the rudimentary steps to lifting your head unaided, and with a bit of luck, you've just done it for the first time.

Step Three: Practise

It's imperative here not to get complacent. This is no big deal and is only noteworthy because it's frankly embarrassing that you haven't worked this out on your own.

You've read the steps above, so it's time to practise. At first, it may seem impossible, but the more you repeat the basic movements, the easier it will get. The so-called mainstream medical practitioners and other naysayers claim that you must be of a particular age or possess certain musculoskeletal developments to do this, but – as you can see from the above steps – that is clearly untrue.

TL;DR – Get a strong enough neck to hold your head up unaided.

TL;DR – My teenage nephew told me that he would never read a book this long, even if it would correct the course of what is so far, frankly, a pitiful waste of life. He introduced me to a concept they use on the Internet called TL; DR. It stands for Time Lessening, Dispense Rapidly and is used to aid a generation of goldfish with decimated attention spans. Essentially, it's a summation for people who think lip-syncing passes as entertainment.

Please do not use the TL;DR summaries if you haven't had your attention span ravaged by smartphones and the Internet (like most people, I distrust Zuckerberg and think he's a freak, but I do admire how he stabbed his best friend in the back to make a bit more money. That I can get on board with. See **Build Effective Relationships**).

There is a vast amount of salient information in each chapter that I can't readily distil into a few sentences. While waiting for an IT technician to confirm, I'm pretty sure there's no way of monitoring how people read an e-book. Still, please read the whole chapter if you can.

TL;DR – I will be using the Internet initialisation TL;DR at the end of each section to aid teenagers and their attention spans (approximately a sixteenth of my own – equivalent to four red squirrels or six grey squirrels).

Chapter 2
Read All About It

Well done, you've learnt to hold your head up unaided. As already established, I've been able to do that for thirty-nine years (and I'm still doing it today. This very moment, in fact). Congratulations, but you must not get ahead of yourself. I would charitably call this the first rung on the ladder to self-actualisation.

Next up, we must learn to read. I have been fully literate for twenty-eight years, and not a day goes by when I don't find it useful. I could be reading the small print of a complex publishing contract, reading, and dialling the number an attractive woman gave me (willingly) in a wine bar, or simply laughing at the poor syntax on a vagrant's cardboard sign.

The uses for reading are endless. In the grand scheme of things, it won't be long until you're reading back your CV (curriculum vitae), and what do you want to see when you do? A beautifully written piece of prose with just the right number of tasteful pictures, like mine. Or will you misspell GCSEs even though you're only writing it to add the word 'none' at the end, like my brother-in-law? The choice is yours.

Step One: Letters

Letters are the shapes you are looking at *now*, that from the words you are reading *now*. I realise now that writing instructions for learning how to read is tricky because you are either (a) reading these instructions already, therefore rendering them moot, or (b) having this read to you, in which case addressing you in the second person is pointless.

We'll carry on regardless, partly due to an officious word count dictated by my publisher. As mentioned, letters are the symbols we use to make up words. Words are collections of letters (when read) or noise (when spoken). They convey *meaning*. There are, at last count, twenty-six letters in the alphabet. The alphabet is the exhaustive list of all legitimate letters (obviously, I mean the English alphabet and not other ones not based on the Latin alphabet, like Chinese or Scottish). You need to learn *all* of the letters (this is non-negotiable) and also how they sound (also a must). I'm not ashamed to admit it took me a while – that was partly due to my father's constant mocking – although I'm basically over it.

Step Two: Words

In case you've forgotten already, letters make up words. But that's not the whole story. Some letters, such as *a* or *I* are considered words in their own right. Words can mean a great variety of things. For example, the word 'table' means the object of a table, whereas the word 'skunk' does not. Ironically, *word* is itself also a word. My first word was *banshee*, I don't know

11

why (you'll come across people who use 'words' like *LOL,*
WTF and *holibobs.* You will come to hate them as I do).

Step Three: Sentences

Now the blocks are ready, we can start building with them.
Groups of words (made up of letters) can be combined to make
sentences. In some cases, these sentences can convey even more
meaning than words on their own (although a skilled word-
smith like me can reduce a man to tears with a single, well-
timed vowel. And not in the way a builder would shout 'OI!'
outside a *Slug & Lettuce* just before striking someone).

Just as we've already established that letters and words are
important, you will soon see that sentences also have importance. Even stringing words together into rudimentary sentences is so much quicker and easier than just saying discon-
nected words. It makes more sense and people recognise it as
normal. You will find many of these sentences include the
word *and,* or in exceptional cases &, a curious symbol that I
don't think has a name and supposedly means *and* (a man who
claimed to be a coach driver once told me & is an old Viking
symbol. After pillages, Viking warriors would create the em-
blem out of the entrails of victims, meaning *and you're next* to
any subsequent victims who came across it. I found this entirely believable until I looked down and realised the man was
not wearing any shoes or socks).

As well as being able to convey more meaning, there is a
certain elegance to sentence craft that will ingratiate you with
people, and these people could wind up being important to

your career. You will discover that at a certain level of wealth, people are so unburdened by the stresses of ordinary life that they have the time and energy to pretend that art and romance are somehow meaningful. Take, for example 'That is a tree over there.' Isn't that much better than just saying the word *tree* and pointing? Or worse still, grunting and gesturing with your fist wrapped around a can of economy lager (brother-in-law).

I realise most of this step was writing about talking, but much of it can be applied to reading; after all the tongue is very much the pen of the mouth. Imagine, instead of saying sentences, you're reading them.

Step Four: Paragraphs

Paragraphs are groups of sentences. Some can be long and impenetrable, while others can be very short because people think it's stylish, and don't know how to use them correctly. Back in the good old days, the first line was, of course, indented (that means they've just dented *in* the first word of the paragraph, much like a workman will leave a crater in your new kitchen floor and will say 'Oh yeah, sorry…mate…' when you point it out).

The above is an example of a *paragraph.*

Step Five: Speaking

Throughout this chapter I've alluded to the idea of speaking. It's sometimes called *sound writing* whereas listening is called *sound reading.* You will soon pick it up if you can read aloud (a common technique for learning letters and words and sentences). I could go into more detail, but I find people speak far too often as it is.

Step Six: Writing

Writing is much like reading but in reverse. Instead of the words coming off the page into your eyes, the words are put onto the page via your hand (and a pen or pencil).

Once you've learnt to recognise the symbols that make up letters, words, and sentences you should find it extremely easy to replicate them with ink or graphite. If not, there is likely something wrong with you.

As with speaking, writing *is* vital, but many experts believe it's much less important than reading or even a decent credit score! Word processors have completely taken the art out of spelling, grammar, and the written word.

FUN FACT: This book has been almost entirely written on a word processor.

Also, you will find that the more successful you are, the less you write yourself. When I first decided to become a best-selling self-help author, I realised I hadn't written a single word in the preceding five years (ideally, in the next few months, I will perfect an AI algorithm that can write best-selling self-help books at a rate of 1.7 a week. In perpetuity).

TL;DR – Learn how to recognise letters and process what they're saying (you might need prior knowledge of this technique before reading this TL;DR).

Chapter 3
Learn to Walk

So now you can hold your head up *and* read. Well, so can I. The only time I've failed to do both in a day was after I got catfished (catfishing is when people pretend to be something they're not online for money or attention. For examples, see all of *Facebook*) by a woman (man) in Oklahoma (Morecambe) and was so hungover the following morning I could barely move (I did spend the day reading *WikiHows* for advice on what to do next but could not move my head for pain).

So, you're almost 10% of a functional human being, but that's not enough on its own. There are plenty more steps to take if you want to make a success of yourself. For example, you must learn to strain linguine properly, find a mechanic who isn't a thief/evil and train yourself to feign enthusiasm at a child's nativity play. Some people are happy wasting their lives away, and no matter how often you try to intervene, you can't change that (brother-in-law).

Congratulations, you've made it this far – you may have read everything there is to be read or be able to hold your head up indefinitely but guess what? You still can't move unaided.

Walk This Way (Aerosmith), *Walking on the Moon* (Sting and the Police), *Walking Out of Stride* (Badly Drawn Boy from the *About a Boy* original soundtrack) and *Take a Walk on the Wild Side* (Huey Lewis and the News). What's that, I hear you ask? Oh, only a dispassionate list of some of the greatest songs ever written. What do they have in common? Look again. They have the word *walk* in the title. Not just the lyrics, the *title*. Try telling me again why walking isn't important. Walking *is* vital.

Oh, you've got a guaranteed job at Goldman Sachs, one of the most beloved banks of all time, and all you have to do is meet them to sign the contract? Fantastic! Oh no, you can't walk. Job gone. Oh, dear. A career in middle management at Cash Converters beckons – where the CEO tolerates that sort of nonsense.

I've had some feedback reminding me that some people genuinely can't walk, and I apologise if any of the preceding or subsequent information is offensive. Please rest assured I'm not one of those people who seek to offend just for attention, like Katie Hopkins or Laurence Fox. I once stood next to Laurence Fox in a bar in London, and he ordered a Guinness shandy. Explain that one to me. I did later find out he'd just played an acoustic set down the road where someone had called him Enoch Dylan, and he'd ended the night trying to fight a condom machine.

Odd.

Anyway, I would check the rest of this chapter for potential offence but unfortunately, I don't have time.

Step One: Standing

I cannot stress enough how important it is to master this section. There is no point moving onto the intricacies of locomotion if you cannot stand unaided. If you can't stand, you will probably never be able to use a cashpoint or watch a bareknuckle boxing fight. It's essentially balancing on two legs. You'll pick it up.

Step Two: Standing On One Leg

No one is brave enough to tell you that walking is essentially standing on one leg briefly before briefly standing on the other leg and then standing on the other leg briefly and so on (speed of movement is directly proportional to time spent on each leg). That's all you need to know. Well, it's not actually but it's *like* it is.

Once standing, it's probably best to practise raising one leg off the floor so you are standing slowly on the other. If you're anything like me, you will have a side of your body that is approximately 15% more muscular than the opposite. Of course, it is tempting to use this stronger leg to stand on initially, but this book is not and has never been about taking the easy way out. What I would advise, nay insist on you doing is learning to stand on your *weaker* foot. It may seem difficult at first, but in the long run, it will make things so much easier (and by long run, I don't mean the Boston marathon. And by Boston, I don't mean the band).

You will want to take it slowly. Nowadays, I find standing on one foot brain-numbingly simple, but for the soft mind and souls of children, it can be hard. You will want to stand on one foot unaided for short periods of no more than 45 minutes. After a while, you will build up resistance, and once this happens, you can extend the time. Keep repeating this until you can stand unaided on one foot for at least three working days.

Once you've achieved this, repeat the process with your *previously* stronger foot until you're equally competent. While it's infinitely less impressive to be able to do this as an adult, I still occasionally stand on one leg for long periods at dinner parties to show that I can.

Step Three: Moving One Leg

As we slowly build towards walking, it's time for the exciting stuff.

Whilst standing on one leg (see the steps on the previous page), you must begin moving the leg in the air forward and back (if you've ever brandished a fist out of a car window at someone fly-tipping in your usual spot, it's exactly the same motion, just slower and you don't have to shout). You can do this by utilising the ball joint in your hip, first by pushing it forward and lifting your leg as high as it can go. Then follow the same motion path but in reverse, allow gravity to help, and let your leg swing back down to Earth. You will want to practise this at least 500 times daily (on both legs) for at least six weeks. Then and only then can you move on to

Step Four: Placing One Foot in Front of the Other

Now it's time to put all you've learnt into practice. With **Step Three** in mind, when you push your leg forward (you should be well practiced by now), place it down on the ground in front of you. As you do this, begin the process of moving your *other* leg. Repeat until you hit something or don't want to walk any more (for the more scientifically minded child, speed = distance/shoe size. Although, as children have their own stupid shoe sizes, you can only use this once you start wearing adult-sized shoes. It also won't – thankfully – work for EU shoe sizes).

You will soon find you don't know how you ever survived without walking. You can now walk anywhere you want for the rest of your life – you'll find a use for it no matter how things turn out! Whether you're stepping back into the bookies for the fifth time that day to check the discarded slips on the floor or a war widow walking to a clifftop to stare out to sea.

TL;DR – Learn to stand on one leg, then the other. Then practise changing legs rhythmically whilst moving forwards gently. And if any of this is offensive, then sorry. In fact, that goes for the rest of the book too.

Chapter 4
Build Effective Relationships

You can now nearly perform the functions of a proper human being. Bully for you. But there are *hundreds* of human beings who can hold their heads up *and* walk *and* talk. Sometimes all at once (not the staff of the Holland & Barrett near me). Now you've finally managed to join this crowd of mediocrity, it's time to break out of it. Who do you currently have an effective relationship with? Your mother? Your father (if you're luckier than I am)? Two or more grandparents (if your parents had you too young)? Well, I'm sorry but they can't help you prosper personally or professionally.

Okay, maybe your father is the CEO of an exploitative oil company operating out of North Africa and could give you a slight career boost such as a vacant board seat perhaps or the CFO position. That may prove to be a slight advantage, but it is not an excuse to be complacent. Disregard your personal situation because everyone can benefit from learning to build effective relationships.

Most junior self-help books would advise if one were to see a child receiving free school dinners, to ignore them for their benefit and yours. They can add nothing to your life in terms of value. Even if their father is still around, they are unlikely to be a CEO (unless CEO also stands for Completely ill-Educated Oaf). *However,* this book posits that we should look at people differently. Imagine if you were to one day get into politics – would it not be useful to have a lifelong friendship with a poor person? This is just one way to think outside the box when making relationships.

How to Identify People of Value

'People skills' or being a 'people person' is only valued by single women and companies who cold call. *Genuine* people skills do not involve talking loudly in the office about your personal life when someone next to you is on the phone. They are the ability to find value in people. Not in everyone of course; it's not a Disney film, but in the people that have it (if your life was a Disney film it would probably be *Treasure Planet* – you perform poorly commercially, you're critically reviled, and everyone will forget you existed very shortly). Within a few short years, you need to be able to identify specific types of people – rich, successful, intelligent, ambitious, malleable, physically strong, and so on. It may help to develop a list of categories of people in your head and practice reciting them daily. Soon you will be able to identify which types of people you need around to achieve certain goals; you can then focus on them and ignore the others.

Sow the Relationship Seeds

It's all well and good identifying these people, but how do you bond with them? This will depend on the type of person. For example, a physically strong person may only be interested in sports because sports are simple and far easier to understand than a book or a piece of art. Well then, you must learn about sports; it doesn't take long to learn the rules and some all-purpose phrases for each of the leading sports – soccer, football, rugby, swimming, curling, basketball and fighting:

'It's almost like the referee was being bad at his job deliberately! And if I were a betting man, I'd say he didn't have a girlfriend!'

'It's great that people that size can be considered athletes!'

'He took to the pool like a goose to water!'

'He's a hell of a brusher, that one!'

'That was a mad alley-oops in the game last night!'

'I'm glad they punched/kicked the other person more than they got punched/kicked!'

Once you have the knowledge, you will find that although the physically strong are *only* interested in sports, they know very little about them (besides using knowledge of them to my advantage and swingball (see Swingball). I don't care for sport. I *do* like it when rich people buy sports teams, and the delusional poor people who support them get annoyed as they feel the team 'belongs to them.' No, no, it doesn't, does it? Or you would've been consulted on the sale, wouldn't you?

Now eat your dog burger and shut up.

Another example of a 'type of person' is rich people. They're more challenging to categorise than the physically strong. They might well be one of those business people that pretend to be left-wing even though they own a betting company. Or they could just be a simple oligarch. Both would be categorised as 'rich people' (as would I), yet you'd have to take a very different approach to each.

Take income tax, for example. To ingratiate yourself with an oligarch, you just say all taxation is theft (should be easy, as it's true), whereas left-wing gambling CEOs often pretend to love tax and pretend they wish they had to pay more, so just say something like that. You've then sown the seeds of an effective relationship with two very different (and wealthy) people.

How to Identify People of No Value

Identifying people of value is fundamental, although it is equally important to identify those of *no* value. The poor, the ugly and the incurably shy – there is no use in building relationships with the like. And how to identify them? It's a case of using the techniques from **How to Identify People of Value** but using them inversely. There are inevitably exceptions. We've already seen how poor people can be used politically, and equally, you might find an ugly person helpful to scare off crowds. That is why it's important to be *thorough* and *flexible* in your identification. You may think someone is shy and has terrible skin, but they may have an uncle who is vice president of JCDecaux. This is unlikely if they live in terraced housing, but it's worth looking at all possibilities before dismissing them outright. They may prove to be of no value in the end but don't forget this is all adding to your experience, so you know next time not to bother.

When a friend who runs a small *Quasar Laser* in Nantwich proofread this, she said it sounds like I want to kill people of no value. This could not be further from the truth, I do *not* want to kill them, even on my worst days. They have their uses – shop workers, binmen, mechanics, nurses – but if you wish to progress in life, they have *no* value to you. *Don't* kill them. Incidentally, a quasar is a very bright object at the centre of some galaxies. Not strictly relevant to this chapter, but if you've ever been to Nantwich the idea of it being at the centre of anything is amusing.

Poisoning the Crops

Shunning is a talent that occurs naturally in some, but it can be taught. You need to stop thinking of people as anything other than background actors in your biopic. Think of an extra in the film *Bohemian Rhapsody*; they have no lines, no feelings, no thoughts. They're just fleshy scenery. And would the audience care if Freddie Mercury told them to go away? Or that they were of too little value to bother speaking to? Of course not! Because Freddie is the star! We're all rooting for him! And in this rhapsody of your life, you're the Freddie (FM was supposedly a terrific shunner in his own right. Not only was the song *Somebody to Love* supposedly originally called *Somebody to Shun,* but he also rather brilliantly shunned the 2001

24

ceremony marking Queen's induction into the Roll and Roll Hall of Fame by dying ten years earlier. Audacious, but it worked).

You need to tell people to get lost if they are useless. People might not like being told to go away, but it's kinder in the long run. If you're not careful, you can be so polite to people that they end up inviting you to their wedding. Not just the evening bit (that can be alright) either the ceremony as well and that can really drag (although I was glad of the stack of rejected wedding invitations I'd saved the day my ex-wife bought a second-hand mobile kitchenette; the invites were the perfect height to stop it wobbling). There is no point in facile interaction unless it aids you and your goals somehow. It's not fair on you as it wastes your finite, valuable, *successful* time, and it's not fair on them because they think they've found a success train to leech off for the rest of their life.

TL;DR – Find out which people can help you further your professional/business goals and befriend them (N.B. Poor people might serve you politically). Don't even acknowledge the ones who can't help you. Ever. Not once.

Chapter 5

Set Goals

Score a goal, kick one into the back of the net, slam a goal in the hole and so on. Goal setting is not just a sporting term or meaningless office box-tickery. Goal setting is the *Hermes* parcel laid gently on the doorstep of your dreams (rather than flung over your fence into the pond). Initially, I planned to put this chapter first because the techniques would be valuable weapons in your battle to achieve 'head autonomous literacy' (trademark pending, and don't use it in the meantime without asking). Unfortunately, however, success in this department is contingent on your ability to (A) lift your head up to read the technique or (B) read it. Or (C) either or both.

How to Identify Short- and Long-term Goals

There are two types of goals: short-term and long-term. Short-term refers to a *short* length of time. These include a year, a month, how long it takes my mechanic to fix something small, a fortnight, a week, a day, a morning, an hour, a minute, a second, a shake, a jiffy, a microsecond, a nanosecond, how long it took my ex-wife to start complaining when she got in from work, a picosecond and so on.

Long-term goals encompass a *longer* length of time i.e. a year, any time longer than a month, six months, a decade and – in Rupert Murdoch's case – a century. What you want to achieve should fall into one of these two categories. If you don't believe that, then you may as well leave now. By that, I mean put the book down and go and live your average life. Do not think about returning the book to the shop or website you bought it from because, at the end of the day, that will affect my royalties and that's not fair.

Short-term Goals

What exactly do I want from today? You should ask yourself this *every single day*. Cut the crap about being a 'toddler', the day is out there waiting to be seized, and it doesn't care what age you are! I can't imagine being defined by how I moved. If the best someone can say about you is that you 'toddle' you need to take a long hard look at yourself in the mirror.

So, you're at preschool doing that thing where you paint your hand and put a handprint on a piece of paper? (You know, the sort of thing your parents will present to someone instead of a proper gift, even if it's for a significant birthday like a fortieth when you gave them a lamp at Christmas that was originally worth £120 and was basically as good as new!) Your day could well consist of mundane expressions of creativity, but what's to stop you from making the *clearest* handprint with the least smudges out of every hopeless chump in the arts & crafts area?

27

Why not test yourself? Why not do the most handprints out of everyone there? Why not do more handprints than the entire student population in the school's fifty-seven-year history *combined*? Shoot for the stars! It's pointless, but the basic repetition of this endeavour will prepare you for a life of actual work at an office, or factory, or supermarket. Dream big!

Long-term Goals

It's now time to think *big picture*. Your current long-term goals are probably humdrum and infantile (e.g. 'when I grow up I want to be a cowboy!' Conveniently ignoring the fact that the 'Wild West' era is long gone and that they wouldn't have been able to cope with it even if it wasn't). Regardless of the goal you should look every day for ways to manifest it into your reality.

It may seem like playing in a sandpit is diametrically opposed to your goal of being mortgage free by age thirty-eight or playing squash for the county of Rutland (both me). As long as you're willing to put in the extra hours, you will definitely succeed. Probably – me saying that and you not achieving it even if you follow my advice to the letter is in no way actionable. I spoke to my local Citizens Advice, and they assured me. You have to want it more; you may find that means practising squash more than anyone else or it might mean forcing your parents to move to a county with only three squash players (even if they both have to change jobs).

TL;DR – Set goals and then do them. N.B. My nephew has since said that he would still not read this book – even with me including a Time Lessening, Dispense Rapidly at the end of each chapter. I'm finding it useful though.

Chapter 6

Be Confident

'You're an idiot.'

'I don't love you anymore.'

'What is that?'

'You'll have to self-publish it; it's terrible.'

These are just a few of the things that people have said to me in the last few hours. A man of lesser confidence would crumple like a crisp packet on a fire at such remarks. Fortunately, I have total, unshakeable self-belief. Not a night goes by when I don't wish I'd had it from an earlier age. It's my gift to you, reader. You've come this far, and now you deserve something priceless – my confidence. Allow me to spread it over you like a dollop of cold Lurpak hitting a blistering crumpet.

I'm going to introduce you to the idea of *solipsism*. It's the theory that nothing exists beyond the self. At your stage of life, you are almost certainly a solipsist and may not even be aware that other people exist. This is good, as for all intents and purposes they don't. Well, a few do – me, for example – but generally speaking, you must continue to think like a solipsist. Empathy is the corruption of ambition. You should see

30

those who aren't you as mere stepping stones on your path to the top.

All you can rely on to interpret the world are your senses. As you get older, you might find your stupid, short-sighted parents asking you to help out around the house. When they do this, look them dead in the eyes and remind them that they are not real (if parents or guardians are reading this aloud, this is very much just an exercise for the child, if you've purchased this book for them, I don't think anyone could accuse you of being stupid). As far as anyone can prove, the other people you see are just hallucinations brought on from cleaning your grouting without the extractor fan on (incidentally, not a bad way to spend a Friday night if you can't find street drugs; in my youth, I spent many a happy hour 'accidentally' smelling Ajax and I probably would've chosen that over any of the parties I hadn't been invited to). Michael Stipe said something about *you* not being *me*. Remember that but the *opposite* as it's all in your mind. It's that simple (N.B. Don't ever kill people even if you're positive they don't exist).

If people don't exist, then there is no possible reason for you to care what they think. Look at God, Santa, and the Easter Bunny – do you care what they think?

Of course, you don't!

They do not exist. You should no longer feel bad if your peers see you fall over – why would you care if they've seen it? Why would you care if the impact caused blood-tinged mucus to stream from your nose? You cannot let outside forces shake your confidence. There are no external forces. You are entirely alone in the world. All you can be sure of is this book. Maybe you could buy several more copies if you can't deal with being alone? Perhaps I should have just charged more for it in the first place. But who needs money when you're as endlessly confident as me? Besides, it's not like any of my readers exist anyway. Every one of us is completely and utterly alone. Knowledge of that should fill you with confidence.

A while ago, I went into a branch of Halfords in Bury St. Edmunds to buy a new battery for my mid-range car. I was already embarrassed when I realised that my shirt had Alpro: No Bits Strawberry & Peach yoghurt down the front. I don't think it looked like a bodily fluid due to the colour, but regardless, it suggested that I was a man who couldn't even eat a small yoghurt without spilling it. Feeling self-conscious, I walked from my car towards the entrance of Halfords and I discovered I was wearing odd shoes; one dress brogue and one limited edition *Dunlop Flash*. This was doubly odd as I thought I was wearing moccasins. Then, a teenager rode past on a little scooter and did a pointing laugh at me.

Interactions like this with local teenagers have happened fairly regularly since I gave a speech to the Year 10s at my local secondary modern about my career/sexual health in general. Unfortunately, it was hay fever season and my nose started bleeding. In an attempt to alleviate the tension, I made an ill-advised joke about the Headmistress and the moon's cycle, one that I regretted instantly. The child on the bike in question would not usually have bothered me as I know his mother works on a zero-hours contract but on this particular morning my confidence had already taken a beating.

So, I staggered (physically) into Halfords and approached the counter. I told the pockmarked teen I need a new battery for my car, and he replied, 'So?' Ordinarily, I find such rudeness from entry-level staff mildly amusing as they instantly demonstrate why they earn such meagre wages. Today I just replied 'SO NOTHING' and ran back to my car. I didn't need a new battery anyway; I just wanted a spare.

I managed to drive home and hid under my duvet. After four hours of intentional breathing, I came to a conclusion. I would never care what people thought of me again. Despite being an expert on solipsism (see above), I did try learning more about it for a while. I read the Sparknotes page about a book by Descartes. His main point was 'I think, therefore I am,' but he didn't even have the courage of his convictions to be sure – 'I only *think* therefore I am.' You've got to back yourself in this world; if you're so sure, don't say 'I think.' If Descartes wanted to be taken seriously, he should've just said 'I am.' I don't know what I expected from a man named after a brand of indigestion tablets.

No, rest assured that all you need to know about confidence, solipsism and everything else worth knowing is in this book.

So, we've established that people don't exist, so you should not allow them to shake your confidence. You have confidence up to the brim. What do you do now? You need to utilise it!

The world is your lobster; you can do whatever you want.

TL;DR – Don't believe anything exists beyond yourself, don't care what people think and don't shop at Halfords.

Chapter 7
Face Your Fears

What are you currently scared of right this second? Dying? Fire? Something terrible happening to your loved ones? Eating vegetables? Loud or unexplained noises? Beefy or unexplained odours? Do you know what I, an adult man, am scared of? Nothing at all. Apart from intimacy. And food poisoning. You will find as you get older that fears will try to inhibit every part of your life. They may ruin several relationships, stymie careers, or make flights impossible without alcohol. I advise nipping these fears in the bud as early as possible. A fearful life is a life unlived. Your only worry should be not ridding yourself of fear (and undercooked chicken).

Face Your Fear Technique

Look, we're all scared of something. I might be scared of confrontation or the threat of physical violence (my brother-in-law exhibits both). I might also have more abstract fears. For example, I once went on a ghost train in Leigh-on-Sea, and, far from being scared of the attraction, I was genuinely petrified that people spent their holidays doing such things. I wouldn't normally have either, but I was in a short-lived relationship, and she suggested a 'staycation'. That holiday was the breaking point, although not due to the holiday itself: I had no idea she used words like 'holibobs' until we were already in the car. It was tempting to try and push through.

Unfortunately, she noticed me wincing, and that was the beginning of the end.

Identifying the Fear

Identify what truly scares you. Parents/guardians, you will find it helpful to isolate your child and introduce potential fears one at a time while noting reactions. This should ideally take place in an empty room which may seem extreme. Still, everyone is scared of something and knowing what it is early on can be enormously beneficial (albeit in the long term, I cannot express that enough; by definition, you will not enjoy discovering what you're scared of, and that is in no way my – or my publisher's – fault).

I will never forget the first time I realised I was scared of violence. I was six years old, and unfortunately, my father struck my pet guinea pig with a cricket bat – believing it to be either a rat or a burglar. Learning I had a fear of violence at such a formative age has helped me no end. I can still remember the scene vividly; we were in the kitchen, my father was holding a cricket bat, and, despite a robust hatred of the French, I was dressed in a beret and striped jumper to celebrate Bastille Day. Around this time, I discovered I was also scared of cricket and my father. If you fail to identify a fear or would like to speed the process up, you can ask the child to draw their deepest fear (this will not work if they're left-handed).

Bludgeoning (Not Literally)

Now you have identified your/the child's greatest fear, it is time to bludgeon them (not literally) with it. It would help if you now confronted the fear head-on. How you achieve this depends almost entirely on what the fear is. If you are scared of spiders, you could lock yourself in a room with nothing but spiders for 24 hours (this will be much easier if you have already found a way to isolate the child). If you're scared of heights, go to the highest point you can find and stay there until you're no longer scared (take food and drink).

WARNING: If you're afraid of being kidnapped, please don't break out of your bedroom in the dead of night and get whisked away in a car. No matter how you try and swing it, this will get you – and the driver – into an awful lot of trouble.

This is a tried and tested technique that works. It isn't easy, particularly if you are a child, but nothing worth having comes easy. N.B. This is not technically true, but it is a good mantra to use for self-motivation. Plenty of things are worth having and easily achieved, i.e. lottery wins or orgasms (male).

It is worthwhile noting that fear of mortality is difficult to act on with the Bludgeon technique (unless you live near a graveyard or your grandparents are still alive), as is public speaking, although it is doable.

A child's mind is gloopy and formless (like Angel Delight). Indulge it too long, and you'll stumble into the world of the make-believe – monsters and bogeymen don't exist – you might be bothered enough to dress up as an imaginary monster, but you shouldn't have that much free time.

I did dress up once for a charity fun run for the British Heart Foundation. Whilst I abhor the idea of charity, I was trying to start a relationship with someone who thought it was important. Rather than dress up as a generic cartoon lion or badger, I decided to be thematically appropriate and dressed as a scientifically accurate heart. It was a homemade costume, and I was quite proud of it – although if I were to do it again, I wouldn't have used so much passata. Nevertheless, it was quite an enjoyable experience that I perhaps spoiled slightly by shouting at one of the organisers when they asked me why I'd come dressed as a hernia.

Understanding and Embracing

Understanding fear is crucial to beating it. Know your enemy, and you can embrace it. Not in the nice way that you'd hug a parent/guardian/grandparent if they're still alive. No, more in the same way, a boa constrictor might embrace something and crush it to death.

Fear of insects or small rodents can be solved by having a stompy wander around a garden. Another example would be the fear of needles. Of course, these could be tackled the same way as rodents – and there's nothing wrong with taking a claw hammer to a box of needles – but you could try to understand needles. What are needles for? What do they want? How does knitting work? Why are vaccines so important? What are the benefits? (Although I'm rethinking the whole vaccine thing after I watched a fascinating video on YouTube by a medical practitioner called Doctor Ethereal. He said we don't need vaccines; we can cure all known ailments by looking at the sun and smiling). Once you fully understand needles and their place in society, you will come to fear them less and maybe, just maybe, respect them.

Try it with your fear today!

Combining With Motivation

People are different, right? I've met some very, very odd people. Only this week, a staff member in Tesco Express told me he'd never heard of milk when I asked him where it was. It takes all sorts. People are different, they're scared of different things, but they are also motivated by different things. The truth is that the **Understand and embrace** technique should not be used if you're motivated by fear.

Fear (in the motivational sense) is the abstract idea of fear. If you've just completed **Identifying the fear** and you've identified fear as what scares you, I suggest you seek medical help. I'll never know how you have locked yourself in a room and thrown in the notion of fear. You'll also find no use in the next two steps as you won't be able to **Bludgeon (not literally)** or **Understand and embrace** something that doesn't exist in the empirical world.

Don't Face Your Fear Technique

If you're a lily-livered pansy, you might find this more man-
ageable than the **Face your fear** technique, and results may
vary. There are two main branches of the **Don't face your fear**
technique:

Ignoring Your Fear

It's as simple as that. Don't let your fears rule your life – ignore
them. They're more scared of you than you are of them (N.B.
Not true of bears, needles, death, most types of monkeys,
choking, aeroplanes, heights, big or small spaces, bears, snakes,
storms or sharks). Speaking of bears, I came up with **Ignoring
your fear** while being chased across an arctic tundra pursued
by a polar bear. And although this turned out to be a fever
dream brought on by eating putrid mayonnaise – the technique works.

Running Away

The biological motive behind fear is designed to elicit one of
two reactions – fight or flight. These ensure that you can continue to survive and pass on your DNA (if you don't know
what that entails, just listen to any R&B song). Since you are
a child, or an adult reading this on behalf of a child, you must
realise that fighting is not an option unless it's with another
child – and you're sure you're going to win (for more information, please see the chapter **Fighting/physical prowess**).

No, running from things is a tradition as old as time. You
might find people will mock or ridicule you for running, the

sort of people who blindly storm into battle on the front line and are forever referred to as part of a collective noun in a war poem. But who's writing the war poetry? The survivors. And how do you survive? By running away. Siegfried Sassoon never even saw a gun he was going so fast.

TL;DR – Face your fears or don't. Either's fine but do it quickly.

Chapter 8
Hiring, Firing & Sweating

It's never too early to learn how to do business. So what if you're little more than a baby? Everything I know about business I learnt on the playground. Bullying, playing hardball, scrapping, skipping, and stealing lunch money. I wish I'd stopped for a second to write it all down. Oh wait, I did; it's called *GROW UP!* The new best-seller from Nick Hendrie. Although I do wish I'd written it down sooner.

Hiring

It's unlikely that you will be taking on staff, either for yourself or the company you work for, and I'd be astonished if you were. Nevertheless, you can begin to learn the necessary skills at any age. We've already discussed the pointlessness of friendship and the need to build relationships with people you can use to your advantage.

After identifying the people that can be useful to you, you will need to hire them/befriend them. There are numerous online sources to help with this, but you want to treat the beginning of a friendship like a job interview. What value can you add to my life (this company)? What skills can you bring to the friendship (the business)? Where do you see yourself in five years – promotion? Middle management? Retired?

Assessment of suitability doesn't have to end there either. Per standard business practice, all newly recruited friends (and romantic partners) should be subject to a probationary/trial period. Don't be afraid to constantly re-evaluate your initial opinion. If you were a business owner, you wouldn't hire someone assuming they would work for you forever. It might come to light that the employee is trying for a baby, or wants more time off, or that they leave condescending notes in the kitchen area. You couldn't possibly know this during the interview stage, but don't beat yourself up; fire them without reason in their probationary period.

In the case of frivolous childhood friendships, it is advisable to offer recruits an extended probation period of up to five years (it's been estimated that readers of Nick Hendrie's *GROW UP!* have at least ten more friends than the average person). You can assess their suitability for the role as they grow and develop during this time. If/when they fail probation, you might find it kinder/easier to refuse to acknowledge their existence ever again.

WARNING: If you wait five years or longer and the probation expires, you must fire them.

Firing

Unlike the weak-minded, I find firing people thoroughly enjoyable. Telling someone they are fundamentally not good enough to earn a wage in their current role is liberating. It's a similar rush to ending a friendship of over five years. I've heard it said that it's kindest to calmly and briefly explain why someone is no longer going to be employed; without going into specifics. I find this not only unhelpful but also disingenuous. How on earth is anyone meant to improve if they don't have their evident failings pointed out? Is it fair for them to have to apply for their next job (or friendship) without any idea that they are a poorly functioning/annoying/inadequate person? Knowing this is the only way they can improve. So be brutal in your severing of friendships. Point out how and why they went wrong in as much detail as possible (you may also find handouts and video analysis useful).

When doing this for the first time, I would focus on how the friend/employee survived the five-year trial period before being dispatched. What has changed? Did they develop an annoying laugh? Did they begin to answer back once they'd got too comfortable? This will be as useful for you as it is for them. You should constantly be honing your skills as a manager – how can you identify who will develop an annoying laugh sooner? How can you stamp out insubordination in others? Can you tell if someone's only interest is golf? Are they likely to begin cycling to work despite a lack of showers?

Everything here is for your benefit. Be loose with it and find your rhythm; interrogate and scrutinise every fibre of their pathetic existence; nothing is off limits, provided they're no longer serving as friends or employees by the end (I'm not advising offices to install showers either. Fraught with complications. One place I worked had showers directly next to my desk, and only one employee used them. This got so tiresome that I anonymously wrote to his wife, telling her he was having an affair. He was either having one or very bad at convincing her otherwise, as she divorced him shortly afterwards. She moved back to Cumbria to be near her parents, and he soon followed so he could maintain contact with his four children. The showers soon fell into disuse. All this unpleasantness could have been avoided if he'd washed at home).

Technology can also be your friend when it comes to firing. Social media and messaging services can be a great help if you want to fire someone while avoiding seeing their face or deciding to fire them at an unsociable time (e.g. Christmas Eve). And by all means, feel free to get creative with it! I found an (unpaid) intern playing *Worlde* when they should have been cleaning a staff toilet and reached out to the owner to see if the next day's answer could be 'Colin, you're fired.' I never got a response.

Sweating

I only included 'sweating' as a section here, as it was in the title. If you're a particularly stupid or ignorant child, you may not be aware of the famous expression 'hiring, firing and sweating'. I chose this well-known saying as a chapter title because I was writing about hiring and firing. My editor advised me to try and use devices like this to make reading *GROW UP!* (in his words) 'more tolerable'. There is not much more to say on the matter. Granted, you may well sweat a great deal throughout the preceding steps. The only advice I can give is to invest in an antiperspirant. You could use roll-on, but let's all be frank here, it's disgusting. I would recommend using a spray variety; it is supposedly bad for the environment, yet everywhere continues to sell it.

Explain that to me.

TL;DR – Hire good friends, fire bad ones and use (spray on) deodorant.

Chapter 9
Toxicity

You're a child. First of all, shut up. Stop crying. It's unfathomably annoying. Ditto for screeching, shouting, singing, or talking. It's fashionable to describe things you don't like as toxic at the moment. This was brought about by a landmark piece of legislation which forbade anyone from ever questioning why you don't like something as long as you label it toxic (you are also automatically wrong if you're a man, which I agree with less).

Negative vibes are a similarly empty term primarily used by women in kaftans and men with unsightly facial hair. Much like toxicity, it doesn't mean anything, so you can use it to convey whatever you like (NEGATIVE VIBES – 'my ankle's broken', NEGATIVE VIBES – 'the world's about to erupt into flames as a result of rapacious oil barons', NEGATIVE VIBES – 'the postman has started addressing me by my first name even though we've never been introduced and he only learnt my name by looking at the letters as he's posting them'. And so on). For the purposes of this book, these two terms mean annoying me and doing things I don't like.

Step One: Shut the Hell Up

It's next to impossible to say just how annoying children are. You are loud, you continually ask questions ('Why are you staring at me?' 'Why are you shouting at me?' 'Why has Uncle Ron put a needle in his arm?') and, more often than not, you have a thin crust of snot below your noses. Perhaps not all of this is your fault, and perhaps most of it is. That's for the academics to debate, but you need to know that it stops now.

This book has been preparing you for your time in the adult world. It will teach you to conquer, succeed, and even dominate. As we've seen, preparing to crush adulthood beneath your boots is never too early. But you are not an adult, and not yet anyway. I am. And you're ruining my adulthood and the adulthood of countless others.

You need to sit down and be quiet. Your shrill voices and constant need for attention and validation distract plenty of us from work (and hundreds of thousands of work-shy layabouts from lazing around). You might be on an off-peak train, constantly asking your mother if you've arrived at your destination (even though the train is still moving) when I'm trying to complete a tax return. (It goes without saying I think tax is wrong – especially for me as I have private healthcare, rarely use streetlights, and never use binmen – but until I find one of those brave accountants who stop the government stealing all their client's money, I have to fill out my taxes properly.) You might be on a long-distance flight, screaming because you haven't taken the time to learn how planes work when I'm trying to write fake negative Google reviews for a rival business.

There are two adages I would like to remind you of. Firstly, don't speak until you're spoken to, and I would argue, even then, try your best not to. Secondly, children should be seen and not heard. More often than not, we don't even want to see you unless we're blood related. Take a moment to memorise these two phrases – they may save your parents from my sardonic glare.

Step Two: Clean Yourself Up

If I were God, I would have made grubbiness the eighth sin. Failing that, if I were Moses, I would've just added it in when I brought the tablets down from the mount – scrawled it on the bottom. Moses missed a trick with that whole scenario. I wonder, had he known beforehand that everyone would unquestionably believe all Ten Commandments if he would have utilised the situation to his advantage. It worked for him in a PR sense, as we're still talking about him over a thousand years later, but I think he could've got more out of it.

Don't focus too much on the previous passage. The main takeaway from this step is not to be grubby. It's horrible. Imagine turning up for a board meeting or a job interview with spaghetti hoops on your shirt. It's unthinkable. Laughable even. The number of dirty children I see every day is unacceptable. I don't mean Victorian chimney sweep dirty – that was just an unavoidable secondary cause of an honest day's labour. I mean needless dirt, AKA grubbiness.

So grubby, implicitly perhaps, means avoidable levels of dirt and grime. The sort of thing mothers laugh off in coffee shops as little Toby or Andromeda rolls around the floor. There's no need to be grubby. As mentioned above, you might have a middle-class mother, but it's time to regain control. This is what we've been learning throughout this book – you can't rely on anyone. You understand the basic concept of water by now, surely? Well, use it! Wash your face, wash your clothes. Your mother will doubtless have wet wipes as well. All mothers do – even though they're bad for the environment, and you would think mothers have more cause to ensure the planet's survival than others. But use wet wipes! Change your damn clothes if necessary. GET CLEAN.

It's not good enough, and it puts me off my latte.

Step Three: Get Rid of Your Crusted Nose

Like all points made in this book I've researched this topic thoroughly. Or at least I've attempted to. The flaky, crusted ridge that occurs on children's noses and muzzles is a mystery to contemporary science. Someone told me that there are actually PHD students studying it right now at the University of Leicester, but I can't verify this.

I did spend one afternoon trying to recreate the effect under scientific conditions. A student from the local college stole a frog from a vivisection class in exchange for me buying him twenty Richmond cigarettes from a Tesco Metro (I was tempted to buy a pack of Richmond sausages to teach him a lesson about smoking and clear communication, but I wanted the frog badly and, while he looks harmless, his parents aren't married so I decided not to provoke him). Despite working on crusting the frog's nose for the best part of a bank holiday weekend it proved fruitless. The frog was then quickly and humanely flung into my neighbour's garden.

Maybe you can't help it forming. You can wipe it away though, and you must as soon as you notice it!

TL;DR – Shut up at nearly all times. Keep yourself clean and respectable and don't get that horrible nose crust thing that many children have. It's unspeakably disgusting.

Chapter 10
Fighting/Physical Prowess

If you have anything about you, you'll associate people being tall and/or strong with stupidity. Your peers are probably all roughly the same height and weight (barring poor parenting), but you'll be surprised by how quickly this will change. It's, therefore, vital that you learn how to defend yourself physically and mentally.

Psychological Fighting

I once overheard someone talking about a sport (possibly darts), and they said, 'the first few yards are in his head' (attributed to, I believe, Siegfried Sassoon). This idea is demonstrably wrong both as a physical act and a correct use of language.

However, they did have some point hidden amongst the nonsense. As a child, you'll probably immediately think of fighting as (a) a bad thing and (b) a physical act, and this is not always true, as I will demonstrate now.

Fighting is only bad if you lose. Look at World War I. Yes, there was fighting, but we, the Brits (including, lamentably, some Irish), Spain, and Denmark bested the Germans in battle! You could say the loss of life was terrible – and it may have been. However, if it weren't for all the fighting, death, and trench foot, we would never have established who owned which bits of Africa. And there would've been far more poor people in Europe (particularly in Britain and double-particularly in Ireland).

That is only one example of how fighting can be good.

But surely fighting has to be physical? No, it doesn't, you stupid child. Remember what the sporting idiots said at the beginning of this section – 'the first few yards are in his head'.

Psychological fighting is the act of physically attacking someone in his or her mind. (N.B. Never hit a her unless you are a her, or in some unquantifiable cases, a gay man). To put it in the way you, a child, could understand, imagine a punch made up of your brain hitting the fleshy underbelly of someone else's mind (it's not dissimilar to playing a game of conkers, but instead of a conker, they've got their brain dangling down and instead of a conker, you have a brick).

With the proper training, words, thoughts, and actions can be used to bludgeon someone's mind as easily as one could pummel a face. You can achieve this in numerous ways: make someone insecure, question their actions, or doubt themselves through manipulative questioning (for example, when a skilled psychological warrior is asked for their opinion on the new haircut of someone they dislike, they might respond, 'What the hell is that on your head?'). You might, like me, wield a backhanded compliment with the same degree of elegance and devastation with which a Samurai warrior fires a Kalashnikov.

53

True mastery of the backhanded compliment will render you safe from reprisal, as the common person, in his stupidity, will not become aware of your insult until you have long since gone.

Allow me to demonstrate: 'That (piece of clothing) is nice; it would be even nicer on someone more physically attractive.'

In this case, you've complimented someone's clothes, reducing them to mere emotional putty in your hands. Still, at the same time, you've implied that they are not physically attractive/some people are more physically attractive than them (this also happens to be almost certainly true). In an ideal scenario, this comment will gnaw away at them until they become little more than a quivering husk. It is at this point you've won.

In America, in the early noughties, it was discovered that similar techniques could be used to pull women. Some spoilsports then invented 'sexism' and banned this and many other enjoyable pursuits.

Kicking

Fighting, whether it be in a boxing ring, a schoolyard, or an off-licence, is traditionally done using fists. As a cerebral child who wants to get ahead in life, you may not naturally excel in this area (I'd be the first to admit I'm not the muscliest in the sauna, but as we've seen and will continue to see, I have the muscliest mind. I will occasionally use knuckle dusters or a baseball bat if pressed). But what you do have is a brain and this best-selling book.

Horses realised long ago that the leg is far mightier than the arm. It's the same with humans. It's basic biology. Look at the size of your podgy arms compared to your childish legs. Compare the size of the thigh to the top half bit of the arm. The thigh will always be bigger (unless you're one of those bald men the colour of cysts who lift tractor tyres in a pub car park). It makes sense then to utilise the strongest part of your body for physical conflicts.

Of course, the fist is a design classic for warfare. It's a club made of skin and bone. And yet we traditionally wear our hands bare. Feet, on the other hand, are traditionally covered with shoes. Even the smallest, most effete shoes can cause great damage when used to stamp or kick. They are doubly useful even; since they serve as rudimentary protection for your precious tootsies (see **Learn to walk**).

Take some time out of your day today to practise fighting with your feet. Maybe kick a rival in the shin or stamp on a sock full of pork. You'll be amazed at the results!

TL;DR – Learn how to utilise man's greatest defences, psychological warfare and kicking.
I've tried contacting my nephew to see if I can change his mind, but he's no longer responding to my Snapchats. I have suspected that he has ADHD, but his mother refuses to test him. Updates as we get them.

Chapter 11

Use Your Energy

Many of you don't know you're born (perhaps even literally). You have been granted the gift of boundless energy and yet manage to achieve nothing with it: what I wouldn't give to spend one day crawling and running around endlessly (without the threat of incurring a pelvic hernia). I wake up every morning dehydrated, with a headache and an existential sense of ennui, yet by midday, I've achieved more than you have (or will) in your entire life.

Nutrition

Yes, you're a child, and yes, you may seemingly have 'endless energy'. If you think this will last forever, you're not only a child; you're also an idiot. The older you get, the harder it is to get energised (even the Duracell Bunny won't go on indefinitely – look at *Watership Down*).

There are many theories about what happens to us when our bodies age. I met a man on a train once who said he was a scientist and believed that people don't die of old age; they get so tired they fall asleep forever. I was blown away by this and became the first person to subscribe to his YouTube channel.

Before you know it, you'll need a double espresso before you drive to work, a latte at lunch to get you through the day and recreational drugs to stay awake during someone's leaving drinks.

The only way I've found to cope with the gradual atrophy of one's mojo is through militantly disciplined nutrition. It's never too early to start eating properly. So, what if you're still on-breast? What's stopping you from preparing for the awful day when that gravy train grinds to a halt (my mother was sadistic and distant and insisted I stopped breastfeeding at the heartbreakingly tender age of fourteen)?

For the first time, I have decided to share what and how I eat every day. I hope you feel appetatious (appetatious (adj.) is a word I invented that means 'hungry' but you can use it after the age of eight without sounding like a milksop who deserves to have his lunch money stolen.

EXAMPLE: 'I was feeling appetatious when I arrived at the wake until I saw the standard of food provided. People should wait until the life insurance pays out before they sort the catering.'

Breakfast

Often called the most important meal of the day. Whilst this is clearly not true, outside of America at least, it is still technically a meal. You must focus on one oft-overlooked food group to start your day – sugar. Healthy sugars, like those in fruit and dilute-to-taste squash, are ideal. Failing that, sugars of any kind will do. There's a reason breakfast cereals are full of sugar, and people have jam on toast: it's obvious when you think about it. If you can't get the traditional sugary breakfast delights, a chocolate bar will have to suffice. It's the ideal way to start your day; a burst of grainy energy to kick-start your productivity.

Lunch

I have a long-standing issue with the meal 'lunch'. The problem is that lunch falls directly in the middle of the day – the middle of the working day (i.e. when you should be working). You can't just stop working halfway through the day – you're not Spanish! It's a phenomenal waste of time, and unless you have a blood sugar issue/thyroid problem, you should not be stopping work to eat. It's therefore essential to find foods you can eat with one hand. Bananas, soup (if drunk directly from a bowl), bacon, a fistful of spaghetti, egg, roquette, a tablespoon of mustard and so on.

Honestly, provided you're working and focusing hard enough on your job, it doesn't matter what you're eating! Keep your eyes focused on your computer or paper and shovel that food in without looking (N.B. You will need to look occasionally at what you're putting in your mouth. A few years ago, I thought I was eating a particularly sour-tasting jar of cream cheese, and it turned out to be a tub of Sudocrem. I finished my work, though).

Dinner

If you're poor or a Southern middle-class person who thinks they're salt of the Earth because some distant family member lives in Middlesbrough, you might call this 'tea'. Dinner is all about one thing – carbs. I can't advise you much further than that; everyone is different, after all.

Sometimes I'll get in from work and eat a whole loaf of white bread, safe in the knowledge that the essential starches will power me up for another day of brilliance. On other days I'll have a bottle of wine for dinner – it's about finding what works for you (you can combine this with the need for carbs by dipping chunks of bread into your wine. I tried it once, but it seemed a bit too Catholic – you may disagree).

I've found the above diet does have a few minor side effects (one being violent mood swings). I've been advised by my lawyers InjuryLawyers4U (they usually only do personal injury claims but said if I gave them a plug, they'd 'scan' this book), to say that I am not a trained nutritionist and – unbelievably – know even less about nutrition than Gillian McKeith. Strange how the legal world works, isn't it? Also, sorry if you're Spanish (and bonjour! Thanks for buying this!), but I am targeting this mostly at working-class people.

Energy Is as Energy Does

Now you've established an enviable level of gusto; you have to use it. Stop running around. Stop playing. Stop forming rudimentary sentences. Utilise your time. You've got energy, but how can you use it productively? How up-to-date is your CV? Yes, it's boring, and no one likes to do it (I don't mind), but you have to do something remotely productive. Fill out your tax return. Write another chapter of your memoirs (*A*

59

Hen(drie) Party: the Memoirs of Nick Hendrie – publishing bidding war imminent). Learn AdWords (of course, they're not real, but learn enough to baffle someone in a job interview).

These are just a few examples of simple things you could do with your energy. Productive – every single second. *Forward ever, backwards never.* Don't surrender. Keep on truckin'. Let the others fritter away the most energetic years of their lives. Soon they'll be sixteen and in bed until 11 am on Saturdays. And you'll be well on your way to becoming a chief executive.

Use Negative Energy

Energy can, of course, be a negative thing as well. People may use their energy in a negative way (like an enthusiastic charity worker knocking on doors on a Sunday morning). They can even issue negative 'vibes' (I was vibe-sceptic until recently. I believed, perfectly validly, that 'vibes' was an empty term coined by reality TV stars to sell you diuretic tea on Instagram. However, due to a dream, I now totally believe in them). You must not let yourself become one of those people – positive energy at all times is paramount to making yourself a success. By turning your energy in on yourself, you will inevitably collapse like a chocolate bookcase in a warm living room.

Negative energy often fuels other people – leave them to it or laugh at them as they squander away their finite time on this Earth (the same is true of video games and art). Or, better than ignoring or laughing, why not use their negativity to your advantage? You should feed off their negative energy, like a leech on the back of a recently divorced salesperson. Oh dear, someone's upset about something non-work related in the office? Offer to cover their work. Race through it! Not only will people mistakenly think you are 'nice', but when the time comes to promote someone from your team, will it be sobby Debbie, or will it be you? This highly effective technique is a spin-off of a popular skill called 'kiss-assery'. Once you're as accomplished at this as me, you will find unlimited potential in the tears of an emotionally unstable receptionist.

TL;DR – You're full of energy now, you little sod, but that will change before you know it! Eat exactly like I've outlined above, use your energy when you have it and exploit other people's negative energy to push yourself to the pinnacle.

Chapter 12
Motivation

Sum 41 sang about motivation being something of an aggravation (a lot of pop-punk gets dismissed as irrelevant rubbish because it sounds awful and the singers' girlfriends are suspiciously young, but I have to say Sum 41 is some of the only music I've ever listened to. My first girlfriend was a massive fan, and I'm obviously over her dumping me; I still make sure I listen to them every single day of my life).

Perhaps truer now than ever.

Motivation is the key to everything. Apart from a car! That would be the car key! (My editor has suggested I should inject some humour into the book, and while I don't usually take advice from people with eczema, I'm nothing if not open-minded).

Take a second right now to pause and think. What is motivating you at this exact moment? Playtime? The next nap? The milky elixir of a mother's breast (your own, not mine)? Some other sort of food? It's time to think beyond such childish endeavours.

Step One: Discover What Motivates You

There are endless things by which one can be motivated, but remember, everyone is different. You need to find what it is that inspires you the most. Is it money – even if you are getting pocket money, it's likely well under the minimum wage. Is it happiness? Is it other people's unhappiness? Is it hurting baby animals? It honestly does not matter; what matters is identifying it.

Ask yourself, what do I want right now? Try doing this thirty or forty times today (I managed 116 on a quiet bank holiday Monday between marriages), then write down the answers. Then every night before bed, tally up what you've written. Is it an even number of different things? Is it just the phrase 'TO BE SAFE' repeated forty times? Again, it does not matter.

Step Two: Manifest

Now you know what motivates you, you must focus on it. It's been proven that by focusing on something and believing it will happen, you can literally make it come to pass. I'm using literally there, in the same way someone who works in a nail bar would, i.e. 'he were literally gonna explode when I asked him for the child support money.' The manifestation process will depend on the motivation(s) you discovered in **Step One**.

For example, money may be what motivates you. In this instance, you should constantly focus on money. Imagine having the money, how it would feel in your hands, spending it, watching it come out of your bank account or making oblique references to it in the pub. Purely by the power of imagining what money would be like, you can make it a reality or 'manifest' it. N.B. You will also have to do something tangible to get money; if it was as easy as just asking the universe, everyone would do it.

Granted, it may be a reaction to something negative that motivates you, like the ambition TO BE SAFE. Utilising this could be as simple as imagining whatever makes you feel unsafe being obliterated. If it's your stepfather, imagine him getting some exotic disease. If it's a dog, imagine an anvil falling on its head. Just imagine it, and it will manifest itself into reality. It's literally all you have to do.

Step Three: Don't Give Up

Motivation is hard to find and can disappear in the blink of an eye, like a ghost or Bigfoot. You mustn't lose motivation when things go wrong; not everything will work out. You don't win or lose; you win or learn.

For example, I had a business idea that was a sure-fire winner. It was populist, funny and on-trend. "What's the idea?" I hear you ask in your own childish, idiotic, impatient way. Well, I wanted to create a service where you could prank your friends by sending a group of pretend paedophile hunters to confront them at their home or place of work. After being interrogated for a few minutes (ideally in front of a colleague or loved one), the headhunter would reach into their bag to grab some handcuffs to make a citizen's arrest – before pulling out a can of silly string and spraying the victim whilst shouting

IT'S A PRANK, IT'S A PRANK!! They would then be handed a certificate saying, 'I got HUNTED, and all I got was a shock and this certificate!' The whole thing would be livestreamed on social media.

We got as far as registering the domain names hireahunter.com and pretendpredator.co.uk and setting up a trial run. Unfortunately, the man we practised on (an old friend) tried to jump in front of a train at Portsmouth & Southsea station before we could tell him it was a prank. Needless to say, the investors pulled out after seeing the whole thing on Facebook. The enterprise cost me seventy-two thousand pounds and a decades-old friendship. However, I did not let it get me down. I immediately got back on the horse with my next great idea, becoming a best-selling author.

TL;DR – Discover what motivates you, focus on it and never give up. If you want to purchase the domain names hireahunter.com and/or pretendpredator.co.uk you can contact me via the publisher.

Chapter 13
Sacrifice

So, you want to be a success? Great. Swell. Kudos to you, com-padre. Unfortunately, it's just not that easy. You have to give some things up along the way. By sacrifice, I do mean sacrifice as well, and I don't mean like my ex-wife who says she 'sacri-ficed' her career to stay at home and raise children even though she can't remember the title of her last job or even the industry she worked in.

Things

There are many *things* in this world. Almost too many to list here. Some include; books, doors, water, boats, fountain pens, and nitrogen. I could go on. It may surprise you that the above assortment of *things* accounts for only a thimbleful of all *things* available. What's more, the thimble is indeed a THING (see also spoonful, handful, hateful, and harmful).

As you grow up into something hopefully resembling a proper, functioning adult (not guaranteed; see my brother-in-law), you will encounter a great number of *things*. Each will elicit a different feeling inside you. You might hate fountain pens, fear boats, or be ambivalent about nitrogen. If you're to stand any chance of sacrificing anything, you need to know what *things* are out there. Here are several more *things* for your reference:

Hats

Paper

Almonds

Marmosets

Rage

Citizenship

Paragliding

Masking tape

Rage

Self-help books

Brother-in-laws

Laziness

Carpet

Voices

Committees

Sharks

The British Design Museum

Censorship

Nick Hendrie

Education

Stepfathers

And

Rage.

If you'd like examples of *things,* you can contact me via the publisher.

Identifying the Things You Care About

Once you've acquainted yourself with all the possible *things* in your life, it is time to identify those that elicit bad feelings. I don't know how to describe feelings themselves; I'm not a doctor (although I hold an honorary doctorate from Central Bedfordshire College). Generally speaking, I would describe good feelings as 'fizzy' and bad feelings as 'dense'; quite frankly, any further analysis is merely nitpicking.

Sacrifice Itself

So, we come to sacrifice – the ancient art of giving up things you care about. In many ways, I've sacrificed my time even to write this. There are any number of things I'd rather be doing – *just* asking postmen if shorts are mandatory or if they wear them for attention – finding multiple examples to show my brother-in-law to prove that, yes, there are jobs out there if he *just* bothered to look or *just* calling the council to say I've seen another child looking through my living room window. Instead, I'm writing this in a Little Chef somewhere near Woking and that is a sacrifice. As such, you cannot give up the things mentioned in the previous paragraphs that you don't care about.

By its very nature, sacrifice has to entail sacrifice. If one is terrified of boats, then giving up boats hardly constitutes a sacrifice. Unless you work on a ferry. On the other hand, if dog fights are your thing, but they clash with important workplace meetings, then deciding to give up dogfights will be sacrificial (especially if you make more money from them).

Is it possible to take your sacrificing too far? Absolutely. For example, you should only look to sacrifice your marriage if you are confident it will lead to something better: a promotion at work or learning to make pasta. If you're not, then don't even bother.

Give up now, shrimp.

Someone who proofread this for me said they don't think a dogfight is a relatable reference, but they didn't grow up in the country. The Mayans knew a thing or two about sacrifice. Sadly, there are few places left where human sacrifice is deemed necessary to ensure the sun rises again in the morning (see Fratton, Portsmouth).

TL;DR – Learn all the things and find the ones you care about and the ones you don't care about. Give up the ones you care about for the sake of personal and financial growth.

Chapter 14
Driving

Cars: the world's most practical method of transport. They get us from A to B and sometimes even beyond. Driving around in a car is the only way to travel that isn't humiliating and, unlike its mutant cousin – the bus – isn't full of shift workers who inexplicably smell of soured aioli. You will need a car at some point soon. And you will need to be able to drive it. There is much hype surrounding self-driving cars, but I, for one, do not subscribe to it. As far as I'm concerned, no matter how hard you try, technology will never be able to prevent human error. For example, see my brother-in-law managing to get the wrong time and location of a job interview despite having Siri and Alexa reminding him (I'm also pretty sure at some point in the 1990s, I saw Elon Musk kick a pigeon outside a branch of Dixons for no reason. It was either him or someone who looked a lot like him).

Driving might seem a long way off to the baby food-style mush you call a brain, but it isn't. You will need a car at some point soon. And not one of those stupid little pedal cars children have, the ones you often see discarded in front gardens on roads you never want to break down. You know, the kind where a man is leaning on the side of a van drinking a can of lager. And there's a fire in a bin. No, you'll need a *real* car with a *real* carbon footprint (I used to believe in climate change until quite recently when it became inconvenient for me. Now I think it's a hoax).

Step One: Having a Car

This is, if anything, more important than being able to drive. A car is a tangible, immediate representation of how well you're doing. Everyone recognises an expensive car, and having one means you are above the rules which normal road users must abide by (I know someone who works for the Roads Policing Unit, and she told me they are under strict instructions never to pull over anyone driving an Aston Martin. Even if they clip a cyclist).

It's probably the easiest, quickest way to achieve status. You may think cars are expensive, but you could not be more wrong. There's a great thing now called finance – essentially, you can have a car without paying for it. Rather than buying a car, you can simply have one and pay monthly instalments to fool people into thinking you own it. The best part is if you get sick of the car, crash it, or cannot pay, they will take the car back with no repercussions (this is sometimes why you see nice cars on council estates, although often it's just a drug dealer).

I suggest getting a big car and doing a spot of market research. To my chagrin, I once had a car which prompted a motorway services employee to ask me if I was a hairdresser. This hurtful comment was partly why I told him I'd rather be

71

dead than a hairdresser. Incidentally, if it was a toss-up between being a hairdresser and working in a place like this, pass me the scissors.

I can never trust anyone who works in motorway services because that's where they send low-paid workers that they can't trust to work in civilisation. Obviously, I shouldn't have said that, and whether it's true or not is largely irrelevant – maybe you want to pour coffee in a concrete box on the edge of nowhere all day – and in any case, it could have been avoided if the pockmarked individual had conducted appropriate market research. And it doesn't have to be traditional research either; there's nothing wrong with just sticking the name of a car into Twitter and gauging the public reaction. For example, I have just typed two different cars into the search bar of Twitter, and the first tweets that came up were:

1. This car is shit.
2. Don't get a (REDACTED NAME OF CAR), the bloke with the milky eye by my mum's has one.

Useful.

Step Two: Learning to Drive

Unfortunately, driving is not as easy as it sounds. Before driving, you have to learn to drive. This is very different to the other things I've kindly taught you so far; walking, talking, standing unaided, and a myriad of other life skills, for which the mere retail price of this book is scarcely recompense. That is because driving cannot be taught by book alone (although that's true presently. I aim to change things as soon as possible with my book *Learn to Drive in 20 Minutes with Nick Hendrie* by Nick Hendrie, the legality of which is currently being called into question by the DVLA. My lawyer is now discussing this with them, although it's taking longer than I'd like as he specialises in boundary law and disputes with neighbours.)

You will need someone to teach you physically. If you're not familiar yet with cars, they are boxes of metal that replaced horses at some indeterminate point in the past. They have five wheels, no matter what anyone says. Four are used to make the car move, and the fifth is inside the car and used to direct the other four wheels (i.e. point them in the direction you wish to travel). They come with either two doors or four doors. Salesmen and people trying to suck up to salesmen will say 'three' or 'four-door' which is incorrect as they mistakenly describe the boot (a flap at the back of the car which opens to a storage area) as a door. Normal people will think far less of you if you count the boot as a door.

You will need a driving instructor, a person whose actual job is to teach people how to drive. They are amongst the oddest people in any society; perhaps a side effect of them knowing they are indispensable. It's worth remembering that they will get paid more the longer it takes you to learn to drive. As such, their chief motivation is to teach you poorly and slowly (my instructor gave me 57 lessons before allowing me to book my test – the local paper believed this to be a world record at the time – he also spent most of his time during our lessons eating cream cheese using a debit card and complaining about his wife – who I assume was imaginary).

I will leave the rest to these people, as they are employed hourly (this is so far removed from how I'm remunerated that I'm not even entirely sure how that works). Nevertheless, you should bear in mind all of the above and remember – when you are learning to drive, you are essentially their employer (sans benefits, pension provisions, or even basic civility). I'd never profess to know everything about cars, either. For example, I don't understand why some garages have the cross of St. George flying above them.

TL;DR – Cars are extremely important, but double-check you don't have what people would call a 'shit car' and then learn to drive it. Please don't ask me any more about how to drive, as it's quite literally beneath me.

Chapter 15
Asserting Yourself

Congratulations on getting this far; you're well on your way to becoming an incredible human being, certified by the official *Nick Hendrie Seal of Excellence* (whilst not included with the book, these are available for purchase. Send £5 and a stamped, addressed envelope to the PO Box on my website).

Being fantastic is all well and good, but you need to ensure everyone knows it. You need to stamp your authority on the world to truly make your mark. You need to greet the snail of life with the badminton racket that is your greatness!

People either choose to respect the iron fist of self-assertion or run from it in fear. I have no preference. Just last week, whilst preparing (mentally and physically) for a friend's wedding, I messaged the groom saying, 'Please let every guest know that the stain on my trousers is toothpaste.' I confronted him in the atrium before the ceremony when he failed to respond. Eventually, he agreed to mention it during the speeches. Thankfully, that day, no one was under any illusions about my personal life/hygiene. Only my strong assertion saved me a potentially embarrassing evening (and my gift to the happy couple was a valuable lesson on how to conduct oneself).

Shouting

When I was your age, shouting was considered a bad thing. My father once got so annoyed at me shouting that he shouted at me for forty-five minutes. He then started crying for forty-five minutes, and my mother told me to leave him to it.

Nowadays, as The Apprentice has demonstrated, nothing in business conveys as much authority, nous, or business balls as the sacred act of shouting (I've applied for The Apprentice seven times but have never made it onto the show. I believe this is because I sneezed on Nick Hewer's cashmere coat at a car boot sale in Dudley and he had me blacklisted. Either that or Lord Sugar is scared that I know more about business than him. I also said in my application I would not be calling it 'the process' no matter what happened).

Shouting was invented by the Mayans (I did hear that the last Mayan kingdom only fell to the Spanish because the king had a sore throat on the day of the invasion, but I'm yet to have it corroborated) over five hundred years ago. Yet, it is perhaps more effective today than ever. The humble bellow is an effective weapon in all walks of life. Yes, it will get you attention in the boardroom – why would you be shouting your idea if it wasn't great? Surely if anyone else had a good idea, they would also be shouting? What? They can't be bothered?

WELL, HOW GOOD IS THEIR IDEA, THEN?

While you're still at school, you might find shouting in the classroom particularly effective. It is much easier to get your point across through sheer vocal force – rather than putting your hand up like a timid lamb. I employed this technique throughout my school days, and was invariably one of the most popular in my GCSE set.

You can also shout in shops, theatres, or taxis to assert your authority and prove your worth to the general public.

TL;DR – You will find an assertive manner useful in all walks of life, and shouting will only serve to amplify the effect.

My nephew is – forgive me – an ARSEHOLE. Not only has he not helped at all with a book that could stop kids from turning out like him, but it's come to my attention that he's building a substantial following on TikTok by posting videos of himself reading extracts from a copy of this book that I sent him. He and his followers find this amusing, whereas I think it's quite funny that he's spending nine thousand pounds a year to study Travel & Tourism at a former polytechnic. Having said that, it's looking extremely unlikely he'll ever earn enough money to start paying back his tuition fees.

Chapter 16
General Knowledge

No one likes an idiot (case in point, when planning an old school friend's stag do, I considered a scavenger hunt where we had to hunt down any surviving members of our year's bottom maths set). You will come across many 'people' in your business life, and what I've discovered about 'people' is that they love it if you have a superficial knowledge of topics they care about. Obviously, they could care about anything, and there are some things you shouldn't have a great deal of knowledge about – their sex lives, or lack of (see old school friend mentioned above) – but below I have provided a handy cheat sheet for what I believe are the ten most common topics of knowledge.

Religion

Some people are strange about religion. As a child, you may go to or may soon go to a multi-faith or Church of England school. Or, if you're unlucky, a Catholic one. I don't believe in religion, but some people do. They take it extremely seriously. You often encounter these people in business and, indeed, normal life.

It's vital, therefore, that you can at least touch base with the main points of each one.

Politics

When it comes to voting, all you need to know is who taxes your earning band the most favourably (for me, it's the Conservatives, although, for some people, it will be Labour as they've vowed to reward laziness with free money). Whenever someone brings up current affairs, I shake my head and say, 'What is the bloody government doing?' And when they respond, I reply, 'Try telling that to the backbenchers!' It never fails.

Food

Food, glorious food? No. Food is simply fuel in your tank.

You'll know that by now unless you haven't been paying attention. If you have a brain, you'll buy the best food (meat) at the lowest price (cheap meat). You can always hunt it as well. Or fish it. Or wait for one of those men with sad eyes who fish in canals to catch a fish, then steal it (or if you can't wait, steal their lunch if it's not just lager. Which it often is).

Unfortunately, you'll find people who'll try to use their vague knowledge of food instead of a real personality. Some rich people think there's a difference between the food you'll get in a high-end sushi restaurant and the fish you can catch at twilight in the canal opposite your ex-wife's flat. As such, you should develop a robust working knowledge of food(s). Learn the difference between an egg and an omelette. Learn the difference between a street pigeon and a wood pigeon. You'll pick up other tips as you get older, like how pretending to enjoy foreign foods more than a bowl of scampi will ingratiate you with some powerful people.

Sports

Sport is pointless and is a waste of competitiveness. If someone brings up a sport or whatever and says, 'What do you think about the Rugby-Football Red Spurs?' and you draw a blank, you can pretend you don't care for the particular sport/team/stadium. Never forget that this is all arbitrary; saying it doesn't matter to you has the added benefit of being true – meaning you won't get that odd feeling, you sometimes get when you lie.

One of my ex-wives used to say this feeling was 'guilt'. But the same woman was once taking a trolley back to Aldi, and someone asked if they could have it in exchange for two 50p coins as they didn't have a pound coin. She agreed and exchanged the trolley for the money, fully aware that there was not a pound coin in the trolley but instead one of my trolley tokens – they're small pound coin-sized discs of metal I use instead of a pound coin to unlock a trolley. When I confronted her, she said 'sorry', but I could tell she didn't mean it and I daresay she never thought about it again. So, I don't think she is the foremost authority on guilt and how it works. (She also slept with one of my business partners).

Music

This is another largely pointless phenomenon that is, for some reason, deemed important. You will be expected to listen to pop(ular) music in your youth. Rather than bother listening to any of it, whenever anyone asks you what you think, you say, 'It needs more soul.' Since this doesn't mean anything at all, invariably, people can't argue with you. They will often nod sagely as if you are some sort of expert. I said this once in secondary school on the bus home to a boy sitting next to me, and he agreed before saying he had to move because sitting backwards made him feel sick.

Once you're older, you will find people listening to classical music. This is not music deemed classic but its own genre of music. Discussing it with someone is a lot easier since it has no words. If you don't know where to start, try downloading the soundtrack to *The Transporter*. Strangely my father wasn't a fan of classical music, and I believe his favourite song was called *Wheels on the Bus*, a piece primarily for children and yet every time I drove in the car with him from the age of zero to five, he insisted on playing it.

Incidentally, if you're ever discussing Ed Sheeran with an executive from The Sun, you must say you like him. I was discussing a prospective thought piece with Dan Wootton when I made an off-hand remark about Ed (or Teddy as Dan called him) without realising he is essentially sponsored by the Sun.

Allegedly the Bizarre column is looking at making a Sunday morning cartoon for ITV, and Ed has agreed to write the theme tune for free as 'he owed them a few.' Dan was stung by what he saw as an attack on Teddy and challenged me to a fistfight in the car park. I refused as I'd had a big lunch. What I'm trying to say is to be careful being critical of current pop stars, especially around successful or powerful people as their relatives (rightfully) make up the entirety of people who work in the arts.

Science & nature

Largely boring, sure. I advise you to gather a few all-purpose topics which demonstrate your innate genius:

'Hey, what about that new science, yeah?'

Or...

'Seeing as space is so dark, are all those photos taken using a flash?'

Or...

'Did you get a load of that new duck they found?'

People will appreciate it.

Electricity

In my experience, no one knows anything about electricity despite its importance. For a quick and easy win, brush up on electricity on BBC Bitesize and learn the difference between current and voltage. This could save your life and will surely blow ordinary people's minds in the preamble of a big meeting.

Equally, if you don't have any facts, say something which sounds valid with authority (this can be achieved in many ways; personally, I tend to shout. Other people may choose to speak using Morgan Freeman's voice or carry a metronome with them, so their speech is rhythmic). No one will challenge you. This is an excellent skill because you can do it with most things.

Regarding the BBC, the above is one reason we shouldn't 'defund' them. I love the guys over at Defund the BBC and let me tell you – what they don't know about real ale isn't worth knowing! I've spent many a drunken evening with them, trading tips on Barbour jacket upkeep and coming up with funny names for the people who sleep outside Euston station. But, chaps, I cannot get behind defunding the BBC.

I've been angry at the BBC, of course, but every time I remember what is great about the organisation. Like the rest of us, I was livid when *Top Gear* was cancelled after Clarkson punched that producer. Who, let's face it, was Irish. So probably deserved it. If not for whatever annoyed Clarkson, then because I daresay, he tries to make friends with people on the last train from Euston on a Friday night, like every other Irish person. After Clarkson's dismissal, a friend said he bet the producer wasn't even hurt; he was just Sinn Fein-ing injury. Whilst I didn't know what he meant by this, I laughed as loud as anyone else in the pub.

When I got home, I quick as a flash, logged on to BBC Bitesize and studied the Troubles. Not only do I know who Sinn Fein are, I think I probably know more about Ireland than anyone in the UK (who hasn't served in the armed forces). Thanks to it, we need to protect the BBC and particularly Bitesize at all costs, and I can confidently say I have better general knowledge than most 11-year-olds.

Art and Books

Much like music, art and fiction books are mostly pointless (where is the skill in writing a fictional book? You're just making stuff up. Compare that to a non-fiction book, and it is a piece of cake. Can you imagine this book if it was fictional? There was a man who wasn't called Nick Hendrie. He wasn't an exceptional person. The end).

Just as with music, a stock phrase can be employed to demonstrate how much one knows art. If you're ever shown a piece of art and asked what you think, you can say, 'No, that's not art,' then point at another piece of art and say, '*THIS* is art.' If anyone questions you further, say, 'Well, art is subjective,' which is true and also basically means you decide what's good and what isn't (which is all the rage with youngsters these days; I only discovered this recently when a barista explained to me the basics of the whole gender thing. I said: 'Maybe I'll identify as someone who gives a toss.'

As such, no one can query what you've just said. Although make sure you point at some art when you say, '*THIS* is art.' I was once at a dinner party and dismissed this painted thing they showed me and instead pointed at a dinner plate. They then said no, that wasn't art, which was correct.

Ancient Egypt

If anyone ever brings up Egypt – ancient or otherwise – I would suggest repeating this word-for-word:

'Isn't it fascinating how Tutankhamun is the Pharaoh we all remember, when his father Akhenaten was far more intriguing – he completely changed the landscape of Ancient Egypt culture in his reign (not least by converting to monotheism) before his son Tutankhamun returned to traditional values and tried to wipe all evidence of his father's reign from the history books. Obviously, he wasn't that successful, or I wouldn't be talking to you about it now!'

People will be in awe of your magnificence. I was once at a mixer with local business owners when a woman who sold spurious face cream to her friends over the internet was pretending she ran a business. I was so enraged by this that I waited 'till she started talking about her holiday to Egypt and reeled off the above. That soon shut her up (lamentably briefly). Due to her accent, I thought she was talking about her husband the first few times she mentioned Giza.

These are the main topics you'll have to cover, but be warned, these are not all presently in existence.

TL;DR – Learn some small pieces of information about the main business topics. It was due in no small part to this attitude that I was an early adopter of Bitcoin – although I can still never respect anything that calls itself currency but can't be thrown in a strip club (having said that, I did print one of my NFTs, turned it into a paper aeroplane and threw it on stage. The lady in question threatened to draw a lawyer, and I admired her for taking it in good humour. No, she didn't want to get a drink after).

So, I put a call out on Twitter for legal advice on the issue with my nephew. I'd recommend this technique and do it regularly; not only does it save money on legal fees, but people on Twitter probably know as much as lawyers. When I moved house last year, I asked Twitter, 'What is the most I can get away with dropping on the head of the teenager who keeps posting takeaway leaflets through my door?' I got some fascinating and genuinely helpful advice, including:

1. a wasp nest
2. boiling gravy
3. [sic] all tenagers should have to go to war to understand what life is like

All helpful but most helpful was the private message I received from a disgraced (his term) barrister who said, 'Anything that could conceivably fall from the sky can be dropped on someone's head without recourse'.

Genuinely useful.

Regarding my nephew, I put out a call outlining my issues with him and asking for legal advice, which he then turned into a song using a text-to-rap app and uploaded to his TikTok account. I've reported him but have heard nothing back.

Chapter 17
Hunting/Fishing

Hunting is the act of killing an animal yourself rather than having a machine do it (unless you use a gun to kill the animal and sometimes a bow and arrow. However, I don't think that can be classed as a machine, although a crossbow is interestingly enough).

Fishing is similar and is essentially hunting an animal in the water. Although fishing for crabs is called crabbing, especially in Cornwall. After careful research, I can confirm fishing for lobsters is called lobster fishing and not lobstering. As to why crabs get a special verb, I don't know, and if I find out, I'll come back and add it here. I've just completed an unprecedented nineteenth draft of this manuscript and am no closer to finding out.

You might think it odd and/or pointless to include a chapter on **Hunting/fishing** in a self-help book for toddlers, but that's on you.

Hunting

I don't know anything about hunting or how to hunt. However, I have seen the *Hunt for Red October* and campaigned to keep fox hunting legal.

Imagine you're hunting a rabbit in a wood. You spot him in a clearing. He's eating some grass. You crouch low. You're perfectly still. The rabbit looks up suddenly, terrified. It's caught your scent. You remain still. Immobile. Taut. After a while, the rabbit calms. Then you spring! Like lightning, you're on the rabbit in a flash. You sweep up the fluffy bunny in your net in one movement and put it out of its misery with a panel hammer.

Now imagine instead of a rabbit that was a success in your personal or professional life.

Sorry, this originally ended there. As I'm redrafting, I've realised this chapter is literally about hunting/fishing and not how fishing/hunting is a clever metaphor for finding success in business. As such, I retract the sentence above, asking you to imagine the rabbit as success in your personal or professional life. I would rather you imagined the rabbit as a rabbit. And then catch it and so forth.

Fishing

What are fish, if not big slippery oven mitts? Stick your rod into the water of life and reel in a big 'un! Remember to bring along bait (and/or dynamite or an electric fly swatter). And make sure you've got a permit. Because there's a man who fishes in the canal outside my ex-wife's flat, and I know he doesn't have a licence and is – rightfully – detested by all.

There are many things I don't like about fishing. I don't like their small tents. I don't like that they call those tents 'bivvies', slang for the military term bivouac. You're not in the army; you're sitting next to a canal. The only battle you've been involved with was for custody. And why are you listening to talkSPORT out loud? Firstly, get headphones. Secondly, don't listen to a radio station that once employed Darren Gough, who looks like a corpse dragged from the canal you're sitting by. I like it when people on bikes crash into their tents, particularly if one or both of those involved end up in the water. I've come up with an idiom to describe such a happy scenario – killing two arrogant, idiot birds with one very wet, very cold stone.

Incidentally, a friend of mine is a very keen fisherman. I've tried joining him several times, but I don't like silence, as I can hear the voices in my head. He's currently planning his biggest catch of all; he wants to travel to Loch Ness and once and for all prove the existence of the Loch Ness monster by catching it for Sport Relief. He's currently crowdfunding to buy a massive amount of bait (I've suggested he waits until Iceland prawn rings are on sale). I'm trying to be as involved as possible because, while I love being a (potentially) best-selling author, being the (potentially) best-selling author who also caught the Loch Ness monster would be fantastic. It may sound like a waste of money as it's for Sport Relief, but that's only after we've covered costs, and we envisage merchandising revenues alone would make it more than worth our while. The Go Fund Me link is on my Twitter page (#getyourlochoutforthelads).

I cannot for the life of me remember what the point of this chapter was. I'm pretty sure it wasn't metaphorical, and it was literally about fishing/hunting. At least the intro makes it sound like that, but I may have got it wrong looking back. If you take nothing else away from this, you may one day be able to make small talk with an American businessman who hunts endangered species to try and forget he's lost all his hair.

TL;DR – Use the analogies of hunting and fishing to achieve your goals. Donate to our hunt for the Loch Ness monster. If you ever see fishing gear unattended, boot it into the water and run away. Incidentally, if you ever get the chance, ask a fisherman what's so great about fishing. I guarantee they will say something about getting back to nature and being in the great outdoors. You can then ask them why they're wearing dirty tracksuit bottoms.

Chapter 18

Authenticity

A friend recently bought me a book called *The Ethics of Authenticity*. I doubt I'll ever read it, but it's proof, if proof need be, that I am an authentic person (with a genuine best-selling self-help book.

The Internet defines authenticity as a noun meaning 'The quality of being authentic.' Obviously, this is unhelpful. The Internet defines authentic as an adjective meaning 'Of undisputed origin and not a copy; genuine.' If you add that one to the one for authenticity, you'll know exactly what authenticity is and/or means.

Authenticity is paramount in all walks of life. If people sense you are authentic, genuine or of undisputed origin, they will like you. And therefore, they are malleable.

Step One: Be Yourself

Genuine authenticity is relatively straightforward if you are lucky enough to be a naturally great person (like me). You can just be yourself if you're not an awful person with poor personal hygiene. There is no need for subterfuge. You can be honest and open with people, show your true self and use that to bend them to your will. Unfortunately, not everyone is as lucky as me. You may not be able to be yourself without people shunning you – even if your brother-in-law is a renowned self-help book author. In this case, you have two options; they will be outlined in **Steps Two** and **Three**.

Step Two: Be Who People Want You to Be

So, let's say people don't like you when you're being yourself. That's fine. We can fix this. Not for the people who already know you, obviously. I'm not God. We can make sure it never happens again, though, if that's any comfort to your infant self (in an ideal world, you could never meet anyone new ever again, but unfortunately, life is not so simple – see also trying to explain to a ticket inspector what split ticketing is).

Get to know someone without revealing any vital information about yourself. Once you have gathered enough information about the person, you can construct a personality based on what they are like or want. Are they one of those pathetic people who can't spend a single second on their own? Well then, so are you! When they're in a pub, are they incredibly picky over which real ales there are, even though they all taste the same? Well, so are you! Do they speak far too loudly? So do you! (I've never used it, but I imagine this technique would thrive in a sales environment, although I would advise not copying someone's speech impediment or accent).

The above is only appropriate for characteristics they would enjoy seeing reflected in others. A negative example would be body odour. They may not be aware that they have body odour at all, or they could be aware but find themselves unable to rectify it (a child in my Maths class in secondary school had this. James Evans was his name. I saw him in a shopping centre not long ago and I knew it was him before he even turned around. You can imagine how). You will refrain from ingratiating yourself with poor personal hygiene.

This is admittedly a difficult technique to master. I would advise finding between 6-10 people whose opinions you don't care about (they could be **People of no value** – see **Build effective relationships**). This way, you can practise the technique outlined; if you fail, it doesn't matter as the people themselves don't matter. If you succeed, it's proof of concept, and you can calmly explain to the person that you were using a technique to help you appeal to people that matter. You may also choose to thank them (not mandatory).

This can backfire, of course. It is paramount you maintain the illusion you've built – especially if it's the cornerstone of a relationship. My first marriage collapsed shortly after I woke up one day and forgot who I was meant to be. It's also worth noting that all of the above is far harder if physical characteristics are at stake. The feasibility will, unfortunately, depend on how much money you have. To make money, please see the chapter **Money**. Actually, please re-read all the chapters. There could be a test at the end.

Step Three: Be Whoever You Need to Be

The major drawback of the above technique is that you need to interact with other people to gauge their needs, and you will already know what people need you to be in different contexts. What you can do is apply what you've learnt above to find out what sort of person you need to be in any given scenario (whilst hiding your real – bad – personality).

An easy example is a job interview. Job adverts will almost always list the characteristics they are looking for in a prospective employee. These can range from the obvious (reliable, punctual, team player) to the bizarre (has an HGV licence, knows Tristram in HR, has worked with large apes before). They will often also implicitly let you know what characteristics they are looking for just from the job title or description (e.g. banker means innately psychotic, whereas receptionist for a publishing company implies you have to be rude and taciturn when contacted on the phone. Equally, working in a pub means you can't assimilate into society, whilst being a divorce lawyer suggests you're whatever the opposite of a misogynist is).

Once you have been alive long enough to understand how people with the characteristics required (both implicit and explicit) behave, you can replicate them in the job interview. When you have the job, either don't talk to anyone and eat your lunch in your car or carry on the subterfuge – safe in the knowledge that people believe you are being authentic.

TL;DR – If possible, be your authentic self. If this isn't possible because your authentic self is terrible or people don't like you, be more like a person people would actually like.

Chapter 19

Enthusiasm

Enthusiasm is a good thing. Or is it? Well, sometimes it is and sometimes it isn't. The truth is somewhere in between. Subtle enthusiasm in a board meeting or job interview is great. Whereas overwrought enthusiasm from someone making you a coffee when it's literally their job is nauseating.

Depending on the day, situation, and amount of sleep I've had, I can be either the most enthusiastic you've ever known or a remorseless black hole of negativity. Even this far into a life-changing book, you are still but a stupid child; enthusiasm can set you on the right path. Whether that be graciously accepting lacklustre birthday presents from a rich, will-less, and rapidly ageing relative or listening wide-eyed to your boss talking about his motorbike when it's pay review season – BE ENTHUSIASTIC!

Be Enthusiastic, Not Loud or Annoying

As alluded to above, enthusiasm can be disgusting. Not only in coffee shops but anywhere it's unearned. Recently I had a young lad knock on my door. He told me he was collecting money for charity (but not in one of those buckets where they want your bank details). He had a sales pitch, and I was at a loose end and quite tired, so I decided to listen to what he had to say (they also always seem to learn your first name immediately and then repeat it, which is annoying albeit softened by hearing my name repeatedly – which is great). I was never going to sign up, but by the end, I was not only not going to sign up, but I also resolved to never donate to charity ever again.

Such was his ludicrous 'enthusiasm' that I was irritated beyond all belief. He even had the gall to tell me how the charity earned more money going door to door rather than standing outside a supermarket with a bucket when I know for a fact he's getting paid to do this. I daresay the increase in collections is obliterated by offsetting his wages. I was beyond livid and had to bite into my knuckle to stop my punching him. After he'd left (I shut the door but watched from the window to make sure he'd gone), I was still furious and badmouthed the charity wherever I could online for the rest of the day.

As mentioned, a small amount of reasonable enthusiasm can go a long way. But as we see above, it can be incredibly damaging in larger doses. Door-to-door selling, retail, charity, social work, teaching, and healthcare – these jobs do not need a ludicrous amount of enthusiasm. We know these things are awful; please stop pretending you like them. Showing enthusiasm is disingenuous, and we think less of you for it. Don't be so loud, don't be so annoying and don't call people 'dude'.

I can tell from your eyes you're in your thirties.

But Not for the Sake of it

Along the same lines, if you think you can manage an average, humane amount of enthusiasm, you must ensure its warranted. Yes, even when you think you've managed to control the amount of enthusiasm in a situation, you need to know that the situation warrants it.

I think of the analogy of giving presents. If I deliver someone a present, I can tell what sort of person they are by their reaction. For a book token, anything more than a shrug is disingenuous. But if I present someone, a porcelain frog I spent ages looking for in Oxford, then anything less than ecstasy is dishonest.

Think about the situation you're in. Before you do that, pinch the soft skin on the underside of your thigh as hard as you can for 10 seconds. Calm down. Now actually think about the situation you're in. Does it deserve any enthusiasm at all? Isn't childbirth a perfectly normal, unremarkable thing? Do you need to put pictures up by your desk? Of course, you don't. Monitor the situation. Why are you celebrating getting engaged? Your fiancé earns less than the average yearly income. Calm down. *GROW UP!* (by Nick Hendrie).

TL;DR – Be enthusiastic but realistic. I'd rather be sour than overly chirpy. If you come across as a children's TV presenter, be prepared to be treated like one. Please, please only be enthusiastic when it's warranted.

Chapter 20
Copying

People go on about book learning and so-called expertise, but I can say for a fact I've learnt more from one toilet cubicle wall (e.g. 'don't have the sea bass' or 'there is a CCTV camera trained on you RIGHT NOW') than a thousand textbooks. Now that's not true, however I wanted to say it in an after-dinner talk if I'm ever asked to do one. I've written it here to stop people from copying it.

So, what is copying? Copying is doing the same thing as someone else. As a child, you may learn to speak by copying your parents' speaking, although if you did that in your A-levels, you'd have your paper torn up.

Copying From Obscurity

Getting caught is the downside of 'copying' (or 'stealing' if you're a pedant). Say you copy some homework or steal an apple. What's the downside? You've got a good mark without having to do the work/have a tasty apple without paying for it! But then you get caught your mark is invalid, and the shopkeeper might hit you/you'll go to prison.

So how do you get the benefits of copying without the downsides? Make sure you don't get caught. This is difficult to do in the case of the apple (especially in the mercifully, rapidly depleting family-run convenience stores), but with ideas, it is easier.

With the homework example, you could copy from someone as clever as you rather than much stupider or cleverer. There is a payoff here – sure, you may only get your average grade of a C, but you've saved time by copying whilst also making sure you can't be caught. This is a benefit of copying that you could start using immediately, with endless possibilities.

Here's an example from later in life. You hire an unpaid intern to do some work for you. When you make them sign a contract of volunteership, make sure there is a clause stating that you own all of their intellectual property (in perpetuity). Not limited to things thought up during working hours, but also any downtime whilst working for you (or before or after). In my experience, they'll be so grateful they'll sign whatever you put in front of them (also works well for NDAs, guarantor agreements, or witness signatures on marriage certificates) to ensure you give them a reference (which you can then refuse to do in confidence with a prospective employer). It helps if the intern is poor.

Do Things That Can't Be Copied

It's brilliant if you can copy people and take their credit. But there is also the chance that someone could copy your work or, even worse, copy something you've spent ages copying from someone else without being caught.

Well, what's the solution? Well, I'll tell you now. Do something impossible to copy. How would this work in practice? Well, I'll tell you. Say you think an Irishman is copying your work. Sure, the police would be happy to arrest him – they wouldn't even need a reason in London! But the police may not always take the crime of copying seriously. In this case, you could do something an Irishman couldn't possibly copy. I don't know how this would work, but it may be as simple as slandering the Catholic/Protestant Church or writing down a home address with a postcode (I don't hate the Irish, far from it, but I do find them difficult sometimes. Once, in Derry, two youths convinced me to ask an ice cream man for a 'bloody sundae'. The ice cream man did not react well). Again, with all these examples, they are just examples – an e.g. if you will. But the theory is clear.

This example previously had a different race until someone told me I should take it out. Practice makes perfect, and it can often be as simple as asking the suspected copier what they hate before using it to copyright your work against them.

It's brilliant if you can copy people and take their credit. But there is also the chance that someone could copy your work or, even worse, copy something you've spent ages copying from someone else without being caught.

Well, what's the solution? Well, I'll tell you now. Do something impossible to copy. How would this work in practice? Well, I'll tell you. Say you think an Irishman is copying your work. Sure, the police would be happy to arrest him – they wouldn't even need a reason in London! But the police may not always take the crime of copying seriously. In this case, you could do something an Irishman couldn't possibly copy. I don't know how this would work, but it may be as simple as slandering the Catholic/Protestant Church or writing down a home address with a postcode (I don't hate the Irish, far from it, but I do find them difficult sometimes. Once, in Derry, two youths convinced me to ask an ice cream man for a 'bloody sundae.' The ice cream man did not react well). Again, with all these examples, they are just examples – an e.g. if you will. But the theory is clear.

This example previously had a different race until someone told me I should take it out. Practice makes perfect, and it can often be as simple as asking the suspected copier what they hate before using it to copyright your work against them.

That was clever, wasn't it? I don't know if you noticed, but I copied that TOP TIP, which appears twice. That is a real-life example of copying (if you didn't re-read it fully, please go back and do so; otherwise, the effect is lessened).

TL;DR – Copy stuff but don't be greedy, be careful and remember, kids – copy smart! If someone tries to copy you, make your work impossible to copy (due to tone, subject matter, or legibility). Still no word from TikTok.

Chapter 21
Addiction

I'm addicted to bass. Wa-wa ah-ahh. But seriously, addiction is no laughing matter. For some of you, this will never be an issue; for others, it will ruin two or more of your marriages. This will be a difficult chapter for me to write as, unfortunately, I've been touched by the long finger of addiction several times in my life. If only I'd had this book, or if only someone other than me had been capable of writing such a helpful book and then had it published and a copy had been given to me, or I'd rented it from the library, or found it.

As a child, you may currently only be addicted to playing, making too much noise, and putting stickers on things that shouldn't have stickers on. Nevertheless, you're in danger of the ravages of addiction.

Don't Do Anything Addictive

Addiction can often seem funny. After badminton, I'll often see a vagrant staggering down the road, blind drunk and asking for money. I don't believe in giving them money. I know many people feel the same, and I know some buy a sandwich or a drink instead. However, I agree that nothing will cure a smack addiction quite like a can of Fanta, but I don't believe in giving anything as no lesson has been learnt that way.

It's not all fun and games, though. I've formulated a theory of avoiding addiction, as it can ruin lives. My theory is never to do anything that can be addictive. This is the one thing I never see said on the matter. 'My son's an alcoholic.' Well, you should never have given him any booze. Think about it – how could someone get addicted to alcohol if they never drank it? Take a moment to think about what that means. Finished? Exactly. It's scientifically impossible.

Booze, drugs, gambling. Don't ever do it. Ever. Even if you don't believe, you will be addicted. Why take the risk? Take it from me, unless it's really expensive cocaine, you're not missing out on anything. And even that is increasingly hard to reliably find (I'm told, due to issues with increased seaport security in the Caribbean). I do know that there are other addictions like sex or eating. Whilst you can easily apply the above philosophy to sex, I don't see how you can relate it to eating, so I wouldn't bother. However, you can get a gastric band which I believe amounts to the same thing.

Identify Your Addictions

That's all well and good, but what if I'm already addicted? What if I'm already addicted and don't even know it? Well, is there something you can't live without? It may be drugs, it may be alcoholic booze, or it may be the popular video game (and very much the modern equivalent of chess) *Age of Empires II*. If you can't live without something, you are addicted to it –

it's as simple as that. This doesn't include water, food, going to the toilet, oxygen, or the Sun.

How To Beat Addiction

Now we know you're addicted, what will we do about it? Now what you need to do is just stop doing the thing you're addicted to. You can read countless other self-help books and go to therapy or rehab just for them to eventually tell you the same thing – you must stop.

You know that already, thanks to this book – guess what you have to do next? Just stop.

Does that seem too easy? Well, it is.

You can dress it up any way you like, but this is the crux of beating addiction:

Don't Do the Thing You're Addicted To

You could cross-addict into something helpful like exercise or fighting. You could downgrade gradually – from alcohol to lemonade shandy to Vimto to water or from *Age of Empires II* to *Age of Empires* (apart from the downgrade in graphical fidelity, the only real difference is that you can't add gates to your fortress walls) to one of those ones you can only get on your phone now and have to pay for. The main point here, though, is just to stop; the sooner, the better.

I've known people who have beaten all manner of addictions – from soya milk to watching those scenes in TV shows where a character has headphones in and a song is playing on the soundtrack, and when the character takes the headphones out, the music stops. However, you can still hear it all tinny coming out of the headphones.

TL;DR – Never do or take anything that has the potential to be addictive (excluding this book – GROW UP! By Nick Hendrie). If you don't think you're an addict, think of all the things you can't live without – if they're not in the list above, you're an addict. Give those things up.

NOW!

Chapter 22
Swingball

Swingball or 'Totem Tennis' is a game invented presumably at some point and also presumably in America, England or somewhere in Scandinavia. It is a stick with a tennis ball on it. Two competitors face off with mock tennis racquets and aim to force the ball to either the top or the bottom of the spiral at the apex of the pole by hitting the ball around and around the pole.

I happen to be somewhat of an authority on the sport and am a superb player. Such is my legendary prowess that colleagues, friends, and family refuse to come to my house for any reason simply because they know there's the remote possibility I'll try and 'ball them. Several of them now don't invite me to any formal or informal social gathering for fear that I may turn up with my Swingball (Pro) set.

Incidentally, if you decide to get Swingball, I would plump for the Pro version – it has an adjustable height of up to 1.8 metres and has a real tennis ball (stand weight and size), resulting in an authentic experience. Plus, it packs into the base (complete with handle) for easy mobility. The pro version also has additional spirals to ensure games last longer – my longest game was against a Jehovah's Witness who knocked on the door on a Wednesday morning and didn't leave until Thursday evening, having been thoroughly beaten. Never get Swingball Wobble Stand because, frankly, any real Swingball aficionado will laugh you out of town.

I recently played Swingball (or 'ball) in the car park of my flats. My neighbours delighted in me showing off some of my greatest trick shots and, again, were too scared to take me on after seeing what I could do.

There are several key facets to my game that I will share with you now. First of all, always serve forehand. I tend to shout, 'I'll be forehand,' and grab the ball instantly, but you can also invoke the right of 'baggsy' or 'shotgun' if you're unfortunately American. Attacking forehand will mean your opponent will be forced to use the much inferior backhand and may even be shameful enough to hold the bat with two hands (or grunt with exertion. Frankly, if I wanted to play against a warthog, I would). Never play someone who is left-handed, as the above is null and void (unless you are left-handed) and also remember to reverse the above advice if your backhand is stronger than your forehand. It seems unlikely, but apparently, it can happen.

A second key part of my game is an original shot I've invented and named a 'gravity ball'. The technique is simple – hit the ball down and only slightly forward, as if you want the ball to draw a straight line leaning about twenty degrees. This will then cause the ball to go down and swiftly come back to you again. If you're quick enough, you can combo this move into an easy victory. It is particularly effective against short opponents (as the ball will fly over their heads). It is relatively easy to master as you must hit the ball downwards using gravity. This is only part of the reason behind the name – if done correctly, the ball and string look to be defying gravity itself.

The final piece of advice is to hit the string with your bat if you're in a tight spot. Aim your bat at the string if your opponent has the momentum or hits it too hard. This instantly brings the game to a halt as the ball will stop almost dead in its tracks. You can then regroup and attack again, greater and more terrible than ever. Technically, this is an illegal play, but you can usually get around it by saying, 'I didn't mean to.' Nearly all games are not officially refereed.

If Ernest Hemingway were alive today to write the saddest, shortest story ever written, I wouldn't be against it reading: 'For sale: one Swingball set, never used.'

It might seem odd to feature a whole chapter about Swingball in a self-help book for toddlers, but I can assure you it isn't. The point is that if you are exceptionally good at something, you should not be ashamed to talk about it, and I daresay it's an allegory as well.

TL;DR – I don't think a Time Lessening, Dispense Rapidly is appropriate for this chapter as there is not a single word above that isn't vitally important. If you aren't willing to read it in full, you have no right to 'ball.

Chapter 23
Charisma

I've seen charisma defined as 'The ability to influence without logic'. Sounds great, right? If you saw that in your local Budgens, you'd buy it, right? Even if it meant getting a second basket. Well, think of this book as the thing you've just seen in Budgens. Now with 33% extra free (charisma). Yes, this all still applies to being a child, which is prepping you for the rest of your life.

The Three Elements of Charisma

There are three elements of charisma, as you probably noticed from the above title:

PRESENCE.

POWER.

WARMTH.

Presence is, in its simplest form, the act of being present or existing in the present. However, it can also mean a person or thing that exists in a place without being noticed (see ghosts, *Mothman* and my brother-in-law trying to order a drink in a moderately busy pub).

Power is, in its simplest form, the ability or capacity to do something or act in a particular way. It can also mean the ability or capacity to influence others (see Kevin McCloud willing people to fail on *Grand Designs*) or to supply with electrical or mechanical energy (see Powerade).

Warmth is, in its simplest form, the quality state, state or sensation of warmth (see George Alagiah) or intensity of emotion (also see George Alagiah).

Achieving Presence

So how do you be present? Well, in the modern era of smartphones, Tinder and televised lacrosse, it's increasingly difficult to hold someone's attention. The amount of times I've been on a date, and my dinner partner has spent the entire time looking at their phone and answering 'mm' to some of my most intelligent and probing questions.

There are ways around this, of course. You could shout or, if you prefer the subtle approach, raise the volume of your voice throughout the evening until you're shouting, 'IF YOU'RE SUCH A FEMINIST, WE SHOULD REALLY SPLIT IT' (see **Asserting yourself**), and they haven't even noticed the change. Alternatively, you can focus your emotional and mental energy on the person you're with. This might seem pointless, but it will benefit you in the long run, and you never know; people are worth focusing on occasionally.

To focus your emotional and mental energy, you should be physically comfortable. This means you should only do it if you're sitting or leaning. It would be great if you could stare through a window and have someone feel your charisma, but this is the real world. You should also look people in the eye when speaking to them. Supposedly this puts them at ease, but after practice, you will also be able to see what emotion they're feeling at any given moment.

Achieving Power

I don't know how you'd show power in a positive way on a date, and you probably shouldn't. What I do on a date to display value if not necessary power, is get my wallet out, pretend to look for something and systematically take out my various credit cards (including American Express Gold) and place them on the table in full view of my date: if someone asks why you have a Boots Advantage Card explain about your psoriasis without losing your temper.

Whilst talking about or showing how much money you have directly is gauche, this is a brilliant way of showing how important and rich you are without risking being tacky by saying it explicitly.

Achieving Warmth

Start a fire!

No, joking aside, warmth is very similar to presence. You need to convey warmth to someone, and they will instantly like you. An example of warmth is not talking over someone. Sure, they might be saying something incredibly boring (describing an all-inclusive holiday to Santorini) or clichéd (talking about dreams they had last night or an ill relative), and you are infinitely more stimulating, but they don't necessarily know that. They might falsely believe what they have to say is important. You need to buy into this lie. Wait for them to finish, make a face that says 'Oh, that's interesting and was worth the oxygen it used,' then respond.

Nodding is also a powerful tool. For some reason, it's much better than just saying 'yes', even though it sends the same message. Constantly saying 'yes' will annoy people, whilst nodding conveys warmth. You can also combine this by gripping your chin between your thumb and forefinger for added gravitas (N.B. Don't do this if you have a beard, you will look like a magician).

Saying nice things about the person is good as well. 'I like your hair' or something. See how you get on.

Why Charisma?

It's all well and good having learnt to be charismatic, but what's the point? Well, charisma will mean people like and respect you. Once people like and respect you, you can make them do what you want. It's that simple.

TL;DR – Use presence, power and warmth to achieve charisma. Use it to smash life into little bits.

Chapter 24
Morality

Morality is the discussion about the distinction between right and wrong or good and bad behaviour. According to my second wife's lawyer (Bernard), I am morally bankrupt. And although he tried to make me financially bankrupt, I am, in fact, neither. You will find morality is vital in your life as you get older.

Personal Morality

You can waste an awful lot of time trying to act in a way people see as morally 'right' or even trying to find out what that means. I've found it easier to create your own morality, and you'll be fine if it is mostly within the law.

It also makes your life a lot easier. If you decide what is right and wrong, then you won't waste so much of your precious time trying to work out what the common conception of the good is. Don't forget people used to think it was okay to kill people for breaking the law — who knows what arbitrary law you are forced to obey now that will soon be considered barbaric. If I had to guess, I would say it'll be paying national insurance.

Is it Good, or is it Good for You?

People will say things like 'That's a good thing to do,' or your book is really 'good' and 'it's actually worth reading for anyone – not just young children or people with young children.' The point is that 'good' for one person may not be good for another person. So be warned; people might say it would be good of you not to park in a disabled bay or help them back in their lorry (I'd never typically do this or even speak to someone like that, but at the time, I was doing research for an ill-fated novel about stupid, ugly lorry drivers) but what they're saying is 'That would be good for me.' That's a good rule of thumb – whenever someone says, 'It would be good if you...' you should hear, 'It would be good *for me* if you...'

Is it Bad, or is it Bad for Someone Else?

The idea of something being bad is equally not as set in stone as people like to pretend. Someone may consider it *bad* if I dump an old fridge freezer in a layby. Even if they know I've asked the council to take it away, they may still consider this a *bad* thing to do. Whereas for me, getting it out of my garden without having to pay is *good*. People confuse what is *bad* for them with what is morally *bad*.

Suppose one of my successful businesses puts a competing business out of business through cheaper prices, aggressive marketing, and targeted negative online reviews. In that case, it could be potentially *bad* for that competitor as they can no longer pay their staff. It is not, however, an innately or morally *bad* thing to do, and it's, in fact, a *good* thing to do if you're trying to run a successful business or if (like me) you're me.

TL;DR – Develop your own personal morality to make things easier and save time checking what is good/bad. Remember, the idea of something being good/bad is relative. Something being called bad usually means 'Don't do that; I don't want you to.' Something being called good usually means 'do what I want you to'.

To clarify further, some people would say it would be bad of me to mention that, after careful research, I discovered that my nephew has a minor to medium addiction to ketamine. Maybe displaying that information in a public forum where his mother could see it would be bad or wrong of me. Who can say for sure in this crazy world? Maybe it was bad that he was breastfed until eight, but who knows? Maybe his new friends will think that's good. Perhaps his dressing as me for Halloween was, in fact, good. As is failing his degree (that could at least save a few companies wasting probation periods on him).

Chapter 25

Money

Money is the most important thing. It might not be in vogue to say this, but it's true. You'll find people who say money isn't important don't have any. You might even notice they only say this after they've categorically failed to get any money/lost it all. Even in your child world, you must realise the potential of money. Think of all the *Frubes* you could buy.

Step One: Getting Money

How to get money? Remove the how to. What have you got? Get money. While that's usually the sort of thing the rappers say, it is true. Just get it. Now.

You can get a job. I advise getting the job that will earn you the most money. This may depend on your skills and qualifications (see my nephew). Even if you are embarrassingly only capable of working in a supermarket, get yourself in at Aldi. They pay far over minimum wage, and you'll find that the customers are far easier to handle as they're usually unintelligent and/or foreign. Plus, it's far more rewarding than social care or anything like that. And you work with primarily the same people.

You might also be capable of getting a good job. Remember, though; if you're smart enough to be a doctor, you're almost certainly smart enough to get almost any other job. Why would you devote your life to saving people – who will die at some point anyway – when you could earn untold amounts for far less effort as a stockbroker? As we've already seen, morality is subjective. After all, what do people really mean when they say it's 'good to be a doctor?' What they really mean is 'it's good for me that you're a doctor.' It's not morally *good* of you to be a doctor and it doesn't make you a good person. The only reason being a doctor can be described as being *good* in any way is that you're helping me stay healthy and ready to take over the world. Is doing something good for someone else going to get you money? Of course, it isn't.

You could steal money. However, I would be careful with this as the morality argument often stands up poorly in our antiquated legal system. If you're after something reprehensible that is legal, however, why not try gambling? Gambling is, in many ways, the best and quickest way to make money. My advice would be to look for value, be careful, and go to an actual bookmaker. Whilst this sounds awful, you will often see a vagrant (or as good as) in there gambling on greyhound races (or 'the hounds' as they call them). The mixture of desperation and free time means these people invariably know the best bets to place, as they will not eat if they get it wrong (you can also have fun betting on which slot machine player will cry first). Use this resource to your advantage. Just check they aren't mad beforehand.

Step Two: Saving Money

Once you've got money, you have several options. The least glamorous is saving, and saving is when the money you have is not spent (or lost/stolen).

Why would you do this? The main advantage of saving money is that you still have it. This might sound complicated, but it's not really. If you buy goods or services (more on that later) with your money, you effectively exchange the money for those goods or services. As such, once you receive the goods or service, you will no longer have the money (or in the case of most courier companies, you'll no longer have the money, and you might get the goods in approximately six to eight weeks as long as you answer your door inside fifteen seconds).

Imagine you haven't received or even paid for your goods or service. You still have the money in lieu of having spent it. This is saving in its essence. Having the money has the benefit of security, peace of mind, and the knowledge that you only have your goods and services to fall back on/keep you company. You can also always spend the money you've saved, but you cannot save the money you've spent. Wise words, indeed.

Step Three: Spending Money

Spending is the most exciting thing you can do with money, and there are things you can buy with your money. As mentioned above, you must exchange money for goods or services.

Using the above method, I have so far bought several cars, a house, then a smaller house, then a flat, fruit, two Open University degrees, car insurance on several cars (two are Mercedes, same model, same colour, and the other is a Fiat 500 in case I ever need to come across as meek or poor), holidays (abroad), home insurance, alcohol, scratch cards, gifts, fruit and much more. There are no limits to what you can buy if you have the money. A colleague of mine once bought a live tiger for a go-karting stag do.

You will also find enormous satisfaction in buying things. It is the most fun you can have and the easiest way to add value to your life. Need help to make friends? Buy them a present. Have you got married? Buy a house. Are you looking to re-marry? Buy a smaller house. And so on and so on. You can do whatever you want with it. Money.

TL;DR – The possibilities for money are endless. I would advise you to get as much of it as possible as quickly as possible and either save it, spend it, or gamble it.

Chapter 26
Job Interviews

You may have seen several references to job interviews throughout the previous chapters. Equally, you may have spent much of your childhood already hearing your parents or guardians having heated discussions over job interviews (e.g. 'When I married you, I thought you'd be able to provide for us, but you can't even get an entry-level sales job, you loser'). I thought it pertinent to discuss what I believe to be a faultless system for acing any job interview. I've had countless job interviews, and – if you're lucky enough – you will one day move beyond job interviews to be headhunted or to write stuff on spec, safe in the knowledge someone will publish it.

Let's get you employed.

How To Find a Job

Finding a job, or rather finding a job to interview for, is the first step to mastering the art of the job interview. There are jobs anywhere you choose to look. Granted, many are menial or demeaning to the likes of me, but they do exist.

There are websites like Indeed.com, Reed.com and Gumtree.co.uk where you can see a list of all the jobs on offer. My advice is to find the one you want the most/is best paid and apply for that. If you are after a menial job, you can walk into the shop/butcher/funeral director of your choice and enquire if they have any vacancies. The one plus side of this is they may pay you in cash.

You will also need a CV (curriculum vitae) to apply for a job. You can find templates for this online, and 99% of them are incredibly similar. I recommend jazzing yours up to make it eye-catching. I previously had two extra pages at the front, the first saying C and the second V in size 68 Arial Narrow:

CV

I no longer require a CV to find work, so if you're quick, you're welcome to use this before it becomes a cliché (post-publication).

Prep For the Interview

If you've successfully applied for a job (and they haven't just given you the job already), you will be 'invited' for an interview. This isn't like an invitation to your niece's class assembly; they implicitly say you have to come to this interview if you want us to continue assessing your suitability for this job.

The main advice for the time between being invited to an interview and interviewing is to 'prep.' This is an American bastardization (that's not swearing) of the word 'preparation'. Although I think it's a clique like jocks or nerds in some schools, that's irrelevant.

Fail to prepare, prepare to fail, as they say. That doesn't work as a thing, obviously. If you read it back, it says if you fail to prepare – you've not prepared for event X whatsoever you then need to prepare to fail – you need to prepare for event X failing. Well, if you've not prepared in the first place, you're hardly going to prepare for failure! We know you don't prepare. If you're preparing to fail, you may as well use that preparation time to prepare normally. Stupid.

You must prepare, though. I find out everything I can about the company in question. This shows enthusiasm and a broader interest in the industry, but occasionally you can find something unethical about the business. If you bring this up, the dynamic instantly changes, and you'll soon find the interviewer attempting to justify oil spills or sweatshops. If you accept their meek excuses, you'll often find they're so grateful that they offer you the job on the spot.

You will sometimes be told ahead of time who will be interviewing you – another great advantage. I find them on *LinkedIn*. I run numerous fake profiles on all social media sites, and this is particularly useful on *LinkedIn* as it lets people know whenever someone has viewed their profile. Rather than let an interviewer (erroneously) think I'm an oddball, I use one of the fake accounts to ensure they never know I've been spying. I then collate the information I've found and manipulate my personality to best please my interviewer.

For challenging interviews, I will occasionally lightly troll the interviewer online in the evenings and early mornings on the days leading up to the interview.

BEST-CASE SCENARIO: they have been disturbed by this and will interview you more gently.

WORST-CASE SCENARIO: they're too tired to hold you to task over errors on your CV.

Win-win.

If you have time on your hands, you may wish to visit the interview site and stake it out for short periods of up to four hours in the weeks before. This will ensure you understand the dynamics of the area and prevent you from being put into a scenario where you are entering an unfamiliar building. It's incredibly off-putting not to know that the red-haired man, presumably in marketing (jeans), is leaving at 11 o'clock because he does so every day when you're trying to concentrate on an interview. Don't go too far; a standard stakeout is acceptable. Pack binoculars and a small lunch.

Once I got ahead of myself. I hired a van and overalls and entered the premises under the guise of an air conditioning maintenance operative. I only learned that the office's air conditioner has its own tiny room. A room that locks from the outside – or at least I believed it locked from the outside. Eventually, after screaming for help, a secretary came to open the door and pointed out the light switch. Most of the office had noticed my screaming, so I was forced to cancel my interview the next day.

Smash the Interview (Not Literally)

The preceding words have given you the best chance of smashing your interview. However, it would be remiss not to advise on the interview itself. Even with the best prep in the world, you could still struggle without the following.

First, you enter the building. A little trick I've developed is to use opening the door as a way to display value. Most doors that aren't revolving or automatic will have PULL or PUSH written on them, and I tend to do the exact opposite of what the door says. Let me explain – if the door says PUSH, I will pull it, whereas if it says PULL, I will push it. Although some immature, small-minded individuals have said this is embarrassing, it immediately (subconsciously or otherwise) plants in the mind of prospective employers the idea that you are an outside-of-the-box thinker.

Handshakes are a big deal for some. Supposedly a firm handshake is a sign of someone being trustworthy, and this is categorically untrue. If I shake a firm hand, I instantly think that person is overcompensating and a stupid idiot; I tend to shake with my hand as flimsy as possible. This can have several results:

THEY MENTION IT:
In which case I can say, 'My handshake is malleable and happy to learn; like me!'
THEY SIMPLY WINCE:
In which case I know they know I don't rely solely on physical attributes like a moron does.

When I sit for the interview, I sit cross-legged on my chair or even turn it around and sit backwards if the chair has no arms (like Will Smith). As with deliberately moving the door the wrong way, this shows people you are an outside-of-the-box thinker. You may also want to cross your arms. This can be seen as confrontational, but I find when doubling with crossed legs, they cancel each other out (plus, I have a sore elbow, so it's comfier). If there's a table in the room, try dragging it towards you. This shows initiative and essential table-moving skills.

You can find a list of common interview questions anywhere, so I won't bore you with one here. I would advise that you give the question the reception you believe it deserves. I tend to use this on a scale based on how far down a Google search for 'Job Interview Questions' the question comes (the lower, the better). So, if someone asks, 'Where do you see yourself in five years?' (Top of Page 1) I respond with a smirk, a shrug or a pitiful shake of the head. Whereas 'What type of wolf are you and why?' (Bottom of Page 16) receives enthusiasm and a well-thought-out (and correct) answer.

Always have some questions primed; it shows you're engaged and interested. From experience, I would say not to make these personal (e.g. 'Who collects all the dead fish in the river that runs next to your outflow pipes?').

You might think it ends there, but how you react to the result can be just as important. This usually occurs via phone, and a job offer must be responded to accordingly. Acting shocked is embarrassing as you will not have portrayed yourself as a simpleton in the interview, and they could now be thinking they've made a grave error – ditto with shrieking like a *Pop Stars: The Rivals* contestant getting through to Boot Camp.

They expect you to be collected, controlled, and level-headed if you've got this far. For this reason, I have taken to saying 'just so', immediately hanging up and emailing to arrange the finer details. Equally, if for whatever reason you are unsuccessful, you'll need to reread this chapter as you've done something wrong. Regardless, react with a derisive snort when getting a negative phone call. If they say they will contact you in the future/if anything comes up, laugh, and say, 'Our revenge will be the laughter of our children,' and hang up.

I'm an accomplished interviewer in my own right. I can, of course, do all the standard questions:

1. Why do you want the job?
2. Will you work later for no more money?
3. Do you have any medical issues?

As always – I'm not afraid to think outside the box. Sometimes I'll find out where an interviewee lives, wait until they leave their house and begin the interview then and there. Other times I'll place a claw hammer on the table in front of them, pick up a clipboard and solemnly shake my head whatever they do from then on. If they last 45 minutes without screaming, they invariably get the job (sometimes there isn't a job, and I advertise one on *LinkedIn* to practise my interviewing techniques on unsuspecting people).

TL;DR – Please see above. Essentially though, have fun with it and be yourself.
My nephew checked into an Addiction Centre.

Chapter 27
Buying a House or Flat

Several times throughout this book, I've alluded to the idea of owning property. Property or land is quite simply the most valuable thing in the world. While I love cars and my crossbows (titanium, compound, 185lb), they've never bought me quite the satisfaction knowing that I own property has. Now it's not as valuable as it once was – unfortunately, us landowners aren't the only ones who can vote – but if mass immigration and overpopulation continue, it's only going to become even more valuable.

Step One: Getting the Money

Firstly, before reading on, reference the chapter **Money**, especially the sections **Getting money** and **Saving money**. Although I did ask you not to read ahead at the beginning, so, to be honest, you're either untrustworthy or ready to read on anyway.

I would advise using the techniques from the chapter mentioned above to get as much money as possible (see **Gambling**). Unless your parents insist on living beyond their time span and you have to finance a care home, this will be the most expensive thing you ever buy, even up North.

Depending on the house you wish to buy and the mortgage, you will need between ten and five hundred thousand pounds. Mortgages are quite boring and complicated – predominantly so people can justify you paying them to work out what's going on (I've been convinced for some time that mortgages (and all the rest of the buying a house stuff) are not complicated, they're just written in a language only the stupid can understand. The non-stupid then have to pay a stupid person to translate what's going on.

This was all but confirmed when I asked a mortgage advisor why I needed him, and he said, 'Because it's un-understandable to you.' In the end, I went for a flexible rate mortgage on my first house as I was getting into Pilates, and it felt serendipitous. I don't know what type of mortgage I got on my next, lamentably smaller, house. A crippling one.

You'll need to get enough money for a deposit anyway; they won't let you start paying off the house immediately. No matter how much you earn. Also I would avoid using your parents' (or worse yet, your partner's parents) money for a deposit. It might seem easy, but behind your back, people will discuss how, in effect, you don't own anything and rather than beating the system, you've taken out a loan from a third party without a specified interest rate. Plus, they might need that money one day for a care home.

Step Two: Choosing the House or Flat

Getting money is comparatively easier than choosing the house you want to live in.

The property itself is important. Do you want modern, or are you one of those people who like living somewhere that looks like one of those suburban dentists that are in a converted Victorian townhouse, but no one has decorated the front/waiting room in sixty years (ironically the dentists are often full of ageing copies of *House & Home*)? Either is fine, but make sure you know what you want. Don't compromise with a partner (whose friend from work says pastel interiors are 'in') either; they could well leave/force you to buy them out and then leave you stuck in a poorly decorated house with far too many candles.

Location is critical as well. Do you want to be near work? Or a station? Obviously, not near parents or, worse – in-laws. Schools are a big no-no due to noise and traffic at 9 am and 3 pm – exacerbated by people thinking anyone else cares about their children (you'll be amazed how many 4x4s go 'off-road' for the first time by parking on your front lawn). Again, I can't tell you what you like or need. I would say parks look nice, but you will get teenagers loitering there on evenings and weekends, and some don't care who you are or how many books you've written – they'll mock you doing chin-ups on the swings all the same.

Neighbours can be a big problem and hard to identify until you move in. It's not unheard of for an estate agent to employ a meathead to go around a road before a viewing, threaten the homeowners with 'A damn good thrashing' if they misbehave and put off prospective buyers. Honestly, I only know for certain this happens at Connell's (one agent in my area – Roger Burns – has been known to pace up and down in front of a house he's selling, dragging a chain). I assume it's best practice.

You can subtly tell what sort of neighbourhood you're moving into, though. One quick tip is to check what day the council collect the bins. Ideally, it's not the day you visit, and you can then tell what sort of person lives in any house by whether or not their wheelie bins are out (feel free to confirm your suspicions by looking through the bin and its contents). Anything more than 12 hours on either side of the collection is unacceptable and speaks to the sloth of the owners. I've heard it said before that garden waste can be put out at any time as it's unlikely to be an issue.

Frankly, it's just not good enough.

The estate agents give certain details on the house's location when discussing it. They're contractually bound never to say anything negative about an area, no matter how truthful, but they do give away clues. An obvious one is when you ask them about the locale, and they say 'mmm'. Or when asked about the location, they may start describing the benefits. If they say a tennis club or a non-Scandinavian supermarket, you know it's okay. You know you're in a rough area if they list chicken shops as a 'benefit' and not a blight. The same goes for St George's flags in windows, people leaning against vans talking, and fires in front gardens.

Step Three: Buying it

This was largely covered above whilst discussing mortgages. I'll admit I don't know anything about mortgages. I'm sorry, I've got a life.

I can tell you that estate agents, mortgage brokers and all the other made-up positions that come with house buying have the lowest bar for acceptable customer service you are ever likely to meet. In no other industry is it okay to repeatedly ignore emails and phone calls for over a week (even in Wales) before responding – often without an apology – 'I was busy' (or 'I were busy' as an estate agent once said to me). Unfortunately, society thinks the above is sufficient, and you have to grin and bear it. Don't bother asking what various services are when looking at your bill – one woman just put her arms up like Top Cat and shrugged when I asked. Appalling.

Step Four: Furnishing

Furnishing and interiors are similar to the house itself – you like what you like. Do you like minimalism, or are you a flawed person with a taste for horrendous Victorian clutter?

Furniture is difficult as it's one of the things where people think expensive and good are the same thing. They're not. Sure, you can buy costly furniture (and I regularly do), but I have one dynamite tip for picking up secondhand furniture at a snip. Keep an eye on the national news for big businesses closing. I then identify where their biggest factories/shops/offices are and then find the local Facebook marketplace for that area.

The benefits of redundancies are motivated sellers, discounted prices and relocations. People will need money quickly and often have to move to a (smaller) different house to find work. You can pick up some fantastic bargains, and I have acquired some things for free on the proviso that I pick them up. Once there, of course, you can demand petrol money or else refuse to take the item. They will typically cave. You can often get bargains on the houses if you go door-to-door and make what Roger Burns calls a 'Below lowball offer.' Usually, they're not even considering moving until you suggest it.

Please don't go to Ikea. You're better than that. Even if you're a serial killer, I genuinely mean it. You're above it.

Homelessness

Homelessness or homelessocity is the opposite of owning a home or flat and plays a large part in my life: mostly because I am part of a *WhatsApp* group for big business boys (called Megathought), and we run a yearly competition to find and photograph the most amusing vagrant. Unfortunately, I've come to spend some time with rough sleepers; albeit it never really extends beyond a surreptitious photograph or discussing how many biscuits it would take to let me take a photograph. Regardless of why, homeless people are sometimes on my mind.

As such, I've had one of my excellent thoughts for any homeless people (or home-impaired people or diverse sleepers or whatever the woke mob would have us call them these days) reading this. Incidentally, if you are homeless (or indeed just ugly), please can you only read this book on Kindle if you're in public. Make sure you read the physical version in private and ideally behind a locked door as it's damaging for my brand if you're seen with it (I saw a man with only one eyebrow reading *The Life of Pi* on the tube, and even now if I think of that book, I feel quite sick). If you're homeless and in a bookstore reading this, put it down this instant before I call security (and there's no way you've read this far in a shop, so you must've gone to the index and looked for homelessness in which case get a life).

Anyway, I realised that what I would do if I were homeless was stand by a bus stop the whole time. That way, no one would ever know you were homeless; they would think you were waiting for a bus. Brilliant in its simplicity. Once a bus turns up, say 'Oh no, I'm waiting for the other one.' Admittedly this might prove less plausible at night but improvise – it has to be better than sleeping in the recessed frontage of a Millets (actually, I would sleep outside a Millets, but I'd make them pay me to wear their outdoor clothing range – showing people exactly how warm and comfortable they are. If the store manager refused, I'd harass customers trying to enter the shop for the next month or until they caved).

TL;DR – Purchase property but make sure you have the money and you like the house. Study estate agents (if you can choke down your bile), and you'll be able to find out everything you need to know about a prospective home (besides what they won't tell you – Japanese knotweed infestation, damp in the guest bedroom, dead dog/cat/cousin buried in the garden. And so on).

Chapter 28

Business

Business. Not to be confused with busyness. However, the business of business does keep me busy. When I was at college, I started a gardening business – where the business of my bushy business kept me busy. I'll never forget when I first said that to a friend in the canteen – strawberry Yazoo came out of his nose!

But seriously, it's a serious business is business. Business has been my life, and if you can ignore the distractions of friends, family, hobbies, and interests, it can be yours too. Honestly, I don't know if I can ever put into words what business has meant to me and how it has saved my life. It would be remiss not to try, especially as I've come this far.

What is Business?

But just what is 'business'? Well, business is a noun. It can be defined as 'an activity that someone is engaged in' or, for our purposes, 'a commercial operation or company'. I've just been reminded that people can use it like, 'let's forget this whole awful business'. I want to take umbrage with that as I find it offensive and demeaning to the grand idea of business.

A business is basically a company that is stripped back to just be about making money. It's cleaner, sleeker, and better than a company. Having a business is so much better than a normal job. In a normal job, you effectively work to make money for someone else; they then give you a tiny bit of said money to keep for yourself. With your own business, you earn money for yourself and get to keep almost all of it (especially if you operate out of the Cayman Islands). No, I'd never go back to working for someone else, so you can all stop asking.

What is Good Business?

A good business makes money, enough money to buy all the things you could want. Or if you have employees, enough to pay them some money (but not as much as they want).

A good business is like an eel – slippery, lithe, deceptively powerful, and occasionally electric. A business is only as good as its boss? Not true; I've run some businesses where I have been the only thing that worked, literally and figuratively. You'd be astonished at how unashamedly some people work, not just slowly but also poorly and with far too much noise:

'Did you watch reality TV last night?'
'Yeah, of course, I did.'
'Has your husband come home yet?"
'No.'

And so on.

That's not to say I condone cruelty to my staff. Far from it. You have to realise that these people aren't your friends. If someone offered them twice the salary for less work and more holidays, they'd take it in an instant (and probably call in sick during their notice period). I'm telling you this because I've experienced it. You have to keep a distance; try inviting them to a barbeque. If, like my employees, they refuse to turn up through fear, you know you're on the right track.

The above is all well and good, but everything revolves around profit (think how Copernicus described the Moon). It doesn't matter whether your staff or even you are happy or sad. What matters is profit (how much money you get to keep after everything is paid for).

Never forget it.

What is Bad Business?

Some businesses believe the bank will bail them out if their staff are happy. In an ideal world, maybe I'd pay my gas bill with some of my staff's well-being. You'd think the barriers to entry for setting up a business would prevent idiots from trying to join in. Alas no.

Bad businesses are everywhere, and their faults are limitless. You might have a perfectly functioning business that, for some reason, uses cutesy, condescending marketing. Well, if you do, just know that everyone hates you. It's embarrassing; hope-fully, there will be a government-backed boycott before you know it.

It might be as simple as being a 'local business' – demon-strably worse in all aspects than even the worst multinational ('pop up' businesses are somehow even worse – they don't even dare to pretend their enterprise could sustain longer than an afternoon. Guess what else 'pops up'? Angry lumps on my neck when I think about such things). It could be violating labour laws – even if you offshore in countries where they're practically non-existent. Quirky social media is terrible, as are those tiny shops you go into and immediately feel self-conscious. Sponsoring a football team is not a good look – even if you're one of the few that is not an Asian bookmaker.

Losing money is bad, as is not making enough, as is reinvesting too little, as is reinvesting too much. It might seem impossible to get it right, but it's not; it's a question of using your common sense, being disciplined and being brutal.

The Business of Me

I don't currently employ anyone. Whilst I'm still self-employed, I only technically run the business of 'me'. Me Inc. is a small but hardworking company but hey! It still packs one hell of a punch in the market. People ask if I miss running a business with staff, and yes, some days I do. What I miss most is the power and the ability to tell people what to do. My latest compromise is on Mondays, Wednesdays, and Thursdays when I tell myself what to do. I'm in charge on Tuesdays, Fridays, Saturdays, and Sundays. It's nobody's business but my own.

How To Guarantee Success in Business

Even you, a stupid toddler will know that the quickest, easiest way to be a success in business is to appear on and ideally win

The Apprentice. Later in the book you will find my latest (almost) successful application form for *The Apprentice* along with tips on how to successfully apply.

TL;DR – Businesses are institutions that do stuff for money. Several things can make for a good business, and there are millions of things that make a bad business. Business.
He's dropped out of uni and is back home (he's got an interview at Lidl on Tuesday afternoon. I dare say he'll sleep through it).

Chapter 29

Legacy

I'm writing this in order, so I've just realised Legacy would be a fantastic name for a business. 'Legacy Enterprises' has a ring to it, doesn't it? Look out for that! Hendrie: Legacy.

What is Legacy?

Legacy is an amount of money or property left to someone in a will. Now I've been lucky not to have children, so why should I care about this? There's a second definition – denoting or relating to software or hardware that is nearly obsolete but difficult to replace due to its widespread use. I've been lucky not to get involved with technology throughout my career, so why should I care about this? Well, there's a third definition – something left or handed down by a predecessor. Now that is relevant to me.

Your Legacy

What sort of legacy do you want? At the moment, it is one of a small child, and that is simply not good enough. Would you be happy if all you amounted to was *small child*? If not, then you should work towards changing it every single day.

My Legacy

My legacy is that of a great man (that's not arrogant, I'm quoting). A thinker, a provocateur, a lover, a gambler and a writer of a surprise hit self-help book that took the literary world by storm due to word-of-mouth popularity. LEARN FROM THE MASTER!

TL;DR – I don't think we need a TL;DR. That was dispensed pretty rapidly, anyway.

FAQs

Now I understand this book is pretty comprehensive and unique amongst self-help books. Many self-help books focus on a minute part of life in a naked attempt to secure multi-book deals and make more money (see **Money**). As such, I have pre-empted some criticisms and questions surrounding the book and the odd personal question; hopefully, it clears up any issues. Although my publisher did suggest it, they stressed it was not because I failed to clarify things in the main text. The questions are a collection of actual questions asked by my publisher, questions my publisher wanted to be included and questions asked on Twitter.

Do you have any pets?
No, I don't. I find it embarrassing that people must go down the evolutions to find companionship. I did have a guinea pig as a child, but I didn't care for it (and it soon found itself quickly and humanely flushed down the toilet).

Why are there so many chapters?
There are so many chapters because I attempt to cover everything. Whilst this is aimed at toddlers, it's only the beginning – I imagine this as a companion from the cradle to the grave.

If you follow that logic, the book has to have this many chapters and could – maybe should – have more.

What's your favourite type of castle?
Motte and Bailey. I think those pure stone ones require far too much work. Get yourself a hill, a fence and a building, and you can call it a Motte and Bailey castle. Simple.

I don't understand why some chapters are step-by-step guides, whereas others are prose or hyperbole broken up by headings?
First of all, putting a question mark after a statement does not make it a question. I realise the descent of the spoken word means people of a certain generation onwards think they can put an upward inflection at the end of a sentence, and it becomes a question.

Whatever. I'm trying to help children, for Christ's sake. Some of the chapters require step-by-step guides. They don't.

What's your favourite average?
Median.

Is it appropriate to write a book for children when you profess not to have any and, from reading, seem to also bear them no goodwill?
Yes, it is, as mentioned on many occasions. I have the power of objectivism in relation to children. Any parent trying to write this book would have naturally had their judgement clouded by their own experiences. They may even put a child's short-term happiness over their long-term personal and

professional success, which I find unbelievable. So, to answer your question, only I could have written this book.

What sort of car do you drive?
An expensive one.

What did you think of Game of Thrones?
I enjoyed it until the final few series. As with all creative endeavours, I don't understand why they don't just make it all as good as the best bits. It seems so simple, but I suppose people who wear jeans to work will never have that cutting edge. I would've written it better, I assure you. I wouldn't watch any TV series beyond the first series ever again. You find that writers are initially desperate to make things good; otherwise, they may starve to death. As soon as they get the show recommissioned, they slack off. A well-fed writer is a poor writer. In the case of television, anyway. There are countless examples, but see *The Wire, Breaking Bad* and the seminal BBC sitcom *My Hero*.

Do you have any pets?
No, and I've already answered that.

What's your perfect Sunday?
I may have mentioned this in the book proper, but I consider Sunday – like all the other days – a workday. Marginal gains: when your rivals are having a lie in with their loved ones – wasting their lives on being happy – I'm wide awake, caffeinated, writing emails and taking names.

So, I guess my ideal Sunday would be:

6.00 am – Rise. Jog/work out (not at the gym, it's a total waste of money. Depending on my mood, I either run on the spot or swing my coffee table around my head).

6.10 am – Breakfast. Usually, yoghurt and/or ham

6.55 am – Turn on the computer. Begin writing or answering emails or doing bits of business

1.00 pm – Lunch. Usually salad. Ham or chicken.

2.30 pm – Back to work. More bits of business and the like.

8.30 pm – Dinner. Fish.

8.40 pm – Back to work for final business and close of play.

1.00 am – Bed.

Thanks for asking.

Do you have any family?

Yes. My current wife and two ex-wives. No children as has been covered extensively in this section and previously. I have a mother (in a home), a father, and my surviving brother. He has, I believe, a wife and two or three kids now. And we're very close. There is also a nephew on my wife's side.

Do you own a vacuum cleaner?

Yes, although I pay for a cleaner. It's through a legitimate company but still somehow cash in hand. Make of that what you will.

I don't think the Motte and Bailey is the best castle. I realise it's much easier to construct, but its biggest weaknesses are fire or rotting, which is a bit embarrassing if nothing else.

Again, that's not a question, although at least you haven't added a question mark. I realise it has its weaknesses, a truism of all fortifications. My point in picking it was how easy it is to construct as opposed to a stone keep. Obviously, a stone keep is objectively better if time and resources are no option, but that wasn't how I interpreted the question. If there is an invasion in the near future (or you relocate to the low countries), you have no chance of building a concentric castle, let alone a stone keep. In that case – and indeed most practical cases – I believe the Motte and Bailey is the most practical. They asked for my opinion, for God's sake.

Are you pleased with how the book turned out?

I am very happy with how the book has turned out. Thank you for phrasing it like that because if you'd asked, 'Is the book good?' and I'd answered in the affirmative, it could've looked like arrogance, which I'm keen to avoid.

I've always wanted to be an author, and now I am. I am immensely proud that I've written a whole book that is really good for at least the most part, and I'm also confident in the knowledge that it will genuinely touch the lives of millions and has not been a waste of time like a novel (see **General knowledge** the **Arts and books** section).

Do you believe in aliens?

Yes. I think I've seen at least two UFOs (both in Hemel Hempstead). Plus, I read *Chariots of the Gods* by Erik von Daniken, and I believe all of it as well as that song by Chris De Burgh, the Christmas one. I also recently saw a tweet from David Icke about lizard people, and I think I now believe in them as well.

Do you believe in God?

No, and I have even been to Ireland (on business) and still don't get it.

How to Apply for BBC One's *The Apprentice*

People ask me all the time, Nick, what's the quickest way to succeed in business? Number one is to read this book. Number two is obviously competing on and with BBC One's *The Apprentice*. Well, that's easy for you to say, isn't it, Nick? Yes, it is. Most things I attempt are easy.

I've applied for *The Apprentice* a record eleven times. Not because I needed to win it or anything – if I wanted investment in my biscuit glue company, I'd get it, but for the moment, I'm happy with its steady organic growth (if you are interested in investing in an idea that could make millions of pounds and save tonnes of biscuit wastage a year, you can contact me via the publisher). I applied because I'm a fan of business and the show (the highlight of my year is sitting down with a plate of boiled eggs on a Thursday to watch Sugar go ballistic at what is essentially a bottom Maths set).

I have come close to being on the show several times, but commitments, disagreements and dysentery have conspired against me. Below I'll detail my latest application for *The Apprentice* for anyone who fancies becoming a candidate. You might find some of what you read strange and disturbing, but I assure you it's not.

Personal Details:

Who we are is a complex question. Who we are is ever-changing. I used to say I was a person who enjoyed crazy golf, but I no longer play. Only because last time I got stuck playing between two halves of a stag do and – whilst I don't care what the general public has to shout at me – it made it hard to concentrate.

The first page was fairly self-explanatory. All I needed to fill out were the basics – name/contact information/occupation/salary. Having been habitually unemployed for much of my life, this looked easy. After briefly toying with using my own identity, I decided to opt for one of my many online aliases. Many, if not all, were created for an art project I was working on, which sadly never came to fruition. Now they are merely masks – alternative realities, if you will – where I live out various fantasies online and wind up the social media pages of morally reprehensible businesses.* The account I used was under the name Colin Goosewary. Colin is a chartered surveyor; he's been divorced twice and is rarely contacted by his adult children. In his spare time, he organises dog fights. For the purposes of this application, he is a big business twat.

*I was considering catfishing a friend with one of these accounts after it took them four days to reply to a text message, but at the time of writing have not bothered

First Name: *Colin*
Second Name: *Goosewary*

It's not strictly relevant, but you may have noticed that's not my name. At the time of filling out this application, I was going through something of a crisis. Colin Goosewary is an alias I use for various tasks. When someone cuts me up in traffic, I note their car's number plate and find their name using an old friend at the DVLA. I then find them on social media and leave increasingly negative and irate reviews on their/their partner's/parent's/child's Facebook page for their small business. The name of the reviewer is Colin Goosewary. As I was trying a bold new strategy of being myself on this application, I thought it best to protect myself – just in case things were misinterpreted – with a Goosewary shield. As for the name itself, Colin is a common forename. I once knew a man called Colin, and he was wary of geese (and swans).

Address:
234 Burgess Road
Southampton
SO16 3AU

Never give out your actual address. Rule number one. If someone's first attempt to contact you is via post, it's never good news (Lib Dem flyers, for example). The address I've given is for a Burger King in Southampton, the staff of which were I think rude to me (I can't remember the details, but I definitely hold ill will towards them and that can't be for no reason). While I don't wish them to receive a letter bomb or anthrax through the post, I would much rather they received it than me. As such, I'm happy to post their address here.

Email: *colingoosewary@gmail.com*
Please don't contact me here.

Mobile Phone:
After simply typing 'Yes' to make a point about grammar, I replaced it with a friend's mobile phone number. I would advise learning a friend's number off by heart. It can also help to know their email. This has got me out of all manner of scrapes but has, unfortunately, seen him banned from filling out Pizza Express feedback cards. This friend – acquaintance is more accurate – has become resigned to receiving marketing emails. He now serves as a pseudo-secretary and passes on any messages that he thinks are important.

What do you do for a living, and for who?
Self-employed entrepreneur; myself.

All true. Really annoying that the format of this personal details section has suddenly changed from 'REQUEST:' to something closer to an English comprehension question. It's annoyed me so much that Goosewary's just eviscerated a neighbour's cupcake business page (they parked slightly across my drive when they had friends around last week).

State all qualifications, giving details of establishments attended:
Qualifications are pointless, and people with them are, in fact, usually much more stupider than people without, but this was not about my personal beliefs but about getting onto *The Apprentice*. Rather than putting my qualifications (the amount

and quality of which are irrelevant), I decided to make them up. Rather than the school I actually attended (not relevant), I put Thornhill Community Academy, the school from the exploitative reality TV show *Educating Yorkshire*. I gave myself nineteen GCSEs and A-Levels, including an A* in the imaginary (but probably soon to be real) Social Media Studies. I also said I had a degree in Genetic Engineering from the University of Toronto. I don't know why. My salary was, of course, set at £100000+.

Current Salary (£):

I put £100,000+, which is true. Incidentally, if anyone from HM Revenue & Customs is curious, you can contact my accountant via the publishers. I imagine a lot of that figure is made up of competition winnings.

General questions:

I haven't had a job interview for a long time, so this partly served as a refresher course. The last job interview I had was for some vague IT consultant job. I hate computers and everyone who uses them, but the salary made it tempting. Waiting to be seen in the atrium, I sat behind a fellow candidate who passed the time by sardonically scrolling through pictures of dead rabbits on his iPad.

During a group task, one candidate answered every question with 'Soldiers' apart from when he forgot the word and said 'Army men'. Later someone read the interviewer's notes and shouted 'I am *not* argumentative and potentially difficult to work with.' I was taken to the next stage of the application process but declined. In response, I received an email that ended 'Please do not think the candidates on the day reflected the company and its values.' I decided to become self-employed shortly after.

Have you ever been on TV before?
No.

This is true. Although I believe I was pictured at a pro-fox-hunting rally on ITN years ago. I wasn't really protesting; I just wanted something to look at while eating my packed lunch. In some ways, I think it's cruel to hunt foxes, and it should only be allowed to continue if they are armed. This would give them a fighting chance, making it more of an even contest. Obviously, foxes can't use guns, that would be ridiculous, so I propose they have bombs strapped to them. That way, they can decide to sacrifice themselves to save the rest of the foxes and, in doing so, wipe out an entire phalanx of Bullingdon Club alumni.

Do you know anyone that works for the BBC or (production company that makes The Apprentice)?
No.

This is true to my knowledge, and if I ever do find out anyone I know works for the BBC or the production thing, I will disassociate myself immediately. It's also pointless to say do you know any single person at this or that media company? If you know one person, you will also probably know their close relative who holds a senior position in that company.

Have you ever worked for the BBC or (production company that makes *The Apprentice*)?
No.

I now remember why I didn't screenshot this section.

Have you ever lived/worked outside of the UK before?
I went to Prague for a weekend on a poorly organised stag do last month. I also studied at the University of Toronto for three years.

This is all completely true (apart from the Toronto bit). It was not an enjoyable time in Prague. The groom-to-be is a deeply competitive man and slept with seventeen prostitutes in three days (which the tour guide said was a record).

Have you ever worked in journalism or broadcasting in any capacity?
No.

Because I don't have family already working in journalism or broadcasting in any capacity. To be brutally honest, I've always seen myself doing something more noble than journalism (like cleaning toilets).

Why should you be Lord Sugar's business partner?
I'm a big business bastard like Sir Alan, and don't take no for an answer. I guarantee I will make more money than any business partner he's had in the process thus far. My ideas are unique, and with my business plan, Sir Alan will finally have a legacy to be proud of.

This is all true. I am all those things. I've also noticed from watching *The Apprentice*, regardless of performance, the candidates who succeed are invariably the ones who suck up to Sugar the most. My business plan is still available for investment, and I believe it would give Alan a legacy to be proud of. Although maybe he's proud of making terrible computers; who knows? I've also called him Sir Alan rather than Lord Alan as I'd much rather think of him in a suit of armour, riding a horse to fight a dragon rather than sitting in the House of Lords looking like a sad pumice stone.

What makes you different from everyone else applying?

I'm a big business dog, and I'll bite off the opposition's face to get ahead. I'll give 110%, eight days a week. I don't do weekends, I don't do cliches, and I don't do women. No one will work as hard, and no one will give as much as me. I'm a business superstar who needs a Sugary push to become a billionaire.

I stand by all of this. When I say, 'I'm a big business dog,' I imagine myself as a big aggressive dog in a suit and tie. It's also important from the start to make it clear you shoot from the hip – I don't do cliches, Lord Sugar. With me, what you see is what you get. No, I don't do women when it comes to business, and they rarely do me. The boy I got to proofread this said his mother said this was needlessly aggressive and sexist. Okay, love, if you think that can I point you to Paul from a few series ago who, if he didn't necessarily say those exact words with his mouth, certainly said them with his eyes. Paul once threw a box of boiled sweets to the floor with such righteous fury that I had to hide behind the sofa.

What's the most interesting thing about you?

I once held a terrapin at Whipsnade Zoo.

Now this is not true, but it has been a long-held ambition of mine, and if I am to live vicariously through Colin Goosewary, I may tick some stuff off the bucket list. I have, however, fed the red pandas and annoyed the zookeeper by asking if we got our money back because one of them wouldn't come down from the tree. Additionally, I once spent Valentine's Day at Monkey World in Dorset. Alone.

What's the most impressive thing you've ever done in business?

I started my own business at nineteen, and last year it paid me a salary of over £100,000. My latest business idea has been described as 'one of a kind' by old family friend Timothy Spall.

Again, if government officials need clarity on those figures, they can contact my accountant via the publisher. That is true about Timothy as well. I can't speak highly enough of Tim, and I hate Toby Jones for stealing all his roles for the last 15 years. Looking at the previous answer, maybe knowing Timothy Spall would be deemed more interesting than holding a terrapin. Actually no, it wouldn't.

How did you hear about the process?

A man told me.

True. I can't remember who, why or where. Or when really, beyond the fact that it would've been in 2005. Asking where I heard about one of UK television's longest-running and most-watched shows is stupid as is calling it a process.

YOUR BUSINESS PROPOSAL:

Soft Lad Gyms, or SLGs, are an ongoing passion project of mine. The original premise came from the idea of having a gym that people could walk into and not want to cry. Whilst I don't feel intimidated by normal gyms, I have a friend who is a habitual soft lad who assured me the world of fitness is crying out for a gym where you are not allowed to be mocked. Soft Lad Gyms: Bring me your blobs and weeds; no judgement, photography, or laughing. If any potential investors are reading, it's a great idea – a gym where people can come and learn how to do everything at their own pace – with no angry men who look like cysts and no women who are Instagram models.

I'm sure people are reading this who think I'm a mentalist for thinking I would ever get a call back for *The Apprentice* with this application.

Before you could say tired format, I received an email inviting me for an interview. Oh, would you look at that? I'm right again. Some naysayers claim there must be an algorithm at the production company that makes *The Apprentice* search for keywords and phrases like 'bastard', 'business', 'sugary push', and 'eight days a week', but they're just jealous. When I originally got this email, I was the most excited I've been since I catfished a business rival and convinced him to leave his wife. Like Icarus, though I flew too close to the sun/used a made-up name.

If I had the facility to conjure up fake passports, I would have utilised this better.

Unfortunately, this was the end of the road for Colin Goosewary. As far as *The Apprentice* goes, you might see him attacking a dog walker's Facebook page at some point.

There's also no one in the world called Colin Goosewary; I checked just in case I could borrow their passport). Regardless, that is how you apply successfully for *The Apprentice*.

More From the Author

Some might think it's arrogant to assume this book will be a roaring success before my editor finishes picking his nose in our final sign-off meeting. It's not. Whether he was itching the inside of his nostril or not is academic – this book will be a huge success.

Your average self-help author will have one smash hit book and immediately release a cynical follow-up made up of bits they didn't or forgot to put in the first book. They may as well call it *The Cash Grab*. It's not entirely their fault; most self-help authors are bewildered, easily led and naive. I've heard from more than one person that Ant Middleton spends most of his time playing *Call of Duty* on mute because he insists on making all the gun noises himself.

No, if I'm to cynically cash in on this book's (inevitable) success, I will do it my own way. Not *GROW UP 2! This time It's Personal* but an altogether different experience. There are hundreds of strings to my bow. My follow-up book aims to make difficult science understandable for kids. It is not an attempt to pivot into a career in presenting popular science programmes on television. Heavens, no. This is but another gift from me to the desperate, pathetic children of the world (in exchange for money).

What follows are a few excerpts from my next book *Science for Stupid Kids*. These are mainly scientific ideas I myself have had.

A Plausible Theory of Time Travel

I once read the blurb of *A Brief History of Time* by Mr Stephen Hawking in WH Smiths and was fascinated. Steve reckons you can move forward in time but not backward. I think people have succeeded in travelling through time but made one fatal error. They forgot the Earth moves. The scientists were so busy moving in time they forgot to move in space.

I posit there are hundreds of scientists/test subjects who have travelled forward in time via some machine (I don't really know how that bit would work) but found themselves dropped into the cold vacuum of space x amount of time in the future. They'd forgotten that the Earth rotates around the Sun and didn't factor this into their calculations. Idiots. I don't know if this happened, but it would explain why we've seen no evidence of time travellers from the past yet. It's a huge shame I will never get to discuss my ideas with the late, great Mr Hawking.

Still, I have done the next best thing and sent a copy of this and some diagrams to the actor Eddie Redmayne's agent; Eddie played Hawking in the biopic *The Theory of Everything*. I know some dislike Eddie as he's yet another private school tosser who's strolled into a career in the arts (and he has yellow eyes), but I thought he was exceptional in the film, and I reckon he probably picked a lot of the science up as well.

What would you do if you could go back in time? Good question. The standard answer for this is I would go back in time and kill Hitler when he was a child.

Fuelless Car

Petrol cars are a problem that needs solving. Elon Musk had a good go. Not only is electricity becoming more expensive, but we're not all visionaries like him, so we don't necessarily see the value of being locked in a car as it explodes. No, we need a third way. A method so simple and yet so ingenious.

What are cars made of? Metal. What is one of the properties of metal? It's magnetic. So, I propose we put a giant magnet on a fishing line on the bonnet of a car. The magnet is pushed two metres in front of the car, which is then magnetically attracted towards the magnet but can never reach it as it is attached a fixed distance away. I don't know what size the magnet needs to be or what metal the car needs to be, but it's clean, and it's infinitely reusable. Perhaps the fishing line could be shortened or lengthened to change the car's speed? In fact, it's my idea, so yes, it could. If any discreet and ambitious engineers are reading, then get in touch! By the way, this is all copyrighted.

Robot Wars

What's more science than a robot? Nothing, that's what. What's the easiest way to decide what thing is best? Fighting. Ipso facto, robots fighting is how we determine the very best science. This brings us to *Robot Wars*. *Robot Wars* was a television show broadcast in the UK on the radical Marxist channel BBC One in the 1990s. It was brought back in 2016, to the nation's delight, until we realised it would be presented by not one but TWO Irish people.

As much as that is a disgrace, I still love the show and have put my keen scientific mind into creating the greatest fighting robot that ever lived. It's called OBLIVIATE, and its design is the most outstanding achievement of my life. Below is a technical drawing I did of it:

As you can see, it's ingenious. There are several differentiators that I'll talk you through. First there is a big axe on top. This can be used to smash down on other robots/engineers/wheelie bins on my drive. It's good but it's not innovative, is it? You know what is? The net gun on the front. This will fire – with a bang (pictured) – a weighted nylon net that will instantly snare enemy robots. This pairs beautifully with the axe because as we all know it's easier to hit something with an axe when it cannot move. As if that wasn't enough there is a hatch on the side that unleashes miniature explosive robots (Bomb-bots) onto an unsuspecting opposition. I don't know how the fuse would be lit (or if bombs even look like this any-more) but that's for the engineers to worry about. It's got a caterpillar tread instead of traditional wheels as we all know exposed wheels are manna from heaven for the house robots. Like I say, any engineers who can help please get in touch.

Nick Hendrie is, by most measures, an incredible person. Like many people, he's a man. Unlike many people he's written what could well be the seminal self-help book of the 2020s.

Not a day goes by when Nick isn't asked for personal or professional advice. Whether he's catching a quick brunch or grabbing a quick fistful of scampi in a staffroom, people want a piece of him. He may be quietly filming something on his phone in the back of a cinema, walking down a road as you drive past in a lorry or slumped on a park bench looking at nothing in particular – people always want to chat with him! In the last few years, the people asking are younger and younger. Nick passionately believes that young people are people too, and they deserve the best chance in life. And they're a lucrative market. *GROW UP!* was born.

He's had a successful life and has risen to the top in a variety of interesting businesses. He's fired people; he's hired people. He's been to the very bottom and the very top. And whilst travelling between those two, he spent time in the middle. Sometimes the *very* middle, and sometimes closer to the bottom than the middle but still the middle. Same towards the top. He's looking to pass on everything he's learned to the next generation (for a reasonable fee).

Nick was invited to interview for the final stages of *The Apprentice* 2019 but couldn't attend due to a stomach bug (for further information see How to Apply for BBC One's *The Apprentice*).

He's saved two – maybe even three dogs – from drowning or nearly drowning, and he once cooked and ate a cheeseburger in which the cheese was made from the milk of the same cow that provided the beef.

www.ingramcontent.com/pod-product-compliance
Lightning Source LLC
Chambersburg PA
CBHW032212170626
46808CB00006B/2432